FIRST HUNTER

KARPOV KINRADE

CONTENTS

FIRST HUNTER

KARPOV KINRADE

KarpovKinrade.com

Copyright © 2018 Karpov Kinrade

* * *

Published by Daring Books

* * *

First Edition
ISBN-10: 1-939559-50-2
ISBN-13: 978-1-939559-50-0

* * *

Printed in the U.S.A.
First Hunter is a work of fiction. All names, characters, places, and incidents are the product of the author's imagination, or are used fictitiously. Any resemblance to actual events or persons, living or dead, is entirely coincidental.

❀ Created with Vellum

DEDICATION

For our little birds
Rose
Ash
Cat
Always for you

IRIS

*T*his isn't what it looks like. I swear. You see, though I may be tied to this wooden beam with unbreakable chains, and yes, though I may be hanging over a boiling pot full of something that smells worse than an angel's anus, I am in complete control. Utter domination. You get the picture. So, don't worry. All children and sensitive souls may read on.

But wait, Iris, you may be saying. What about those three old crones, Iris?

How kind of you to be concerned.

But those ugly witches stirring the pot and seasoning me with pepper are no problem. Let me introduce you. There's Al'Kallach, the Devourer. Then Ma'Ga'Ta, the Deceiver. And Jane the... um, well there isn't much to say about Jane, to be honest. Except perhaps that her mother disliked her.

They call themselves the Three Sisters, because the Fates was already taken, and the Evil Trinity has a trademark pending. Now I know what you're thinking. Iris, where did you learn all this? You don't hang with that kind of crowd, and you're right, I don't. I learned all this from them... because they've been blabbering for the past three hours.

You'd think they'd cook me already and get it over with, but nooo... Al'Kallach says the pot must always be preheated to five hundred degrees just as their mother taught them. In case you can't tell, I'm rolling my eyes. Now I'm blinking. Rapidly. Because the steam is hot and drying out my cornea.

"Jane," I ask, tilting my head at her. "I've heard so much from your sisters, but I'm thinking it's time we focus on you now. And let's skip all that normal mumbo jumbo I can get off Facebook. I want to get to know the real Jane. What dreams swirl around in that little head? What secrets lie in that cold heart?"

She turns away shyly, cheeks flushing red. "Me? I don't... I don't have any secrets."

"Oh, come on Jane. You can tell me. I mean, who am I gonna tell, right?" I glance at the boiling pot filled with chunks of lizard tail and bat wing.

"Oh... I'm not sure."

"Come on, Jane. Please? It'll make me happy. I hear happy meat tastes best."

She side-eyes her sisters, then shrugs. "Oh, alright."

Bingo.

Crones are a level five monster. Powerful, but not particularly smart, making them very run of the mill. You may be wondering: Iris, why is an awesome hunter like yourself after three average monsters? Good question. But I am not here for them. I am here for someone else.

Oh, Iris, who can it be—

Patience, little bird, patience. All will unfold in time.

Now back to Jane, who is so damn good at stirring that pot, I mean, check out that form.

"Me and Elias," she says proudly. "We're a thing now."

Huh, not what I was expecting. I nod. "He's your bae?"

Al'Kallach scoffs. "If Elias is your bae then I'm a mermaid."

"Shut up," yells Jane. "Shut up, you old hag." She raises her ladle, spraying hot stew on my shiny black cloak. The heat singes, but worse, that's my favorite cloak.

"No. No," says Ma'Ga'Ta the Deceiver. "You are both too tall. Elias like his woman small. Elias like me."

Oh, boy, here we go. "Ladies please, calm down. Relax. We're all women here. No reason for us to fight each other over a man. Am I right? I mean, it's not like Elias is even here?" I let the question hang between them.

They freeze. Jane blushes. "Elias is upstairs." Then she adds with a cheeky grin. "In my room."

Score. I knew he was close, but not that close. Elias is a level ten monster (some would say eleven but eleven doesn't exist) and number one on the most wanted list. Who's the best hunter in the world? Huh, huh?

Al'Kallach hisses in fury at her sister, like she's the one being cooked alive, except, oh yeah, that's me. Ma'Ga'Ta's jaw drops, eyes bulging in her face like bowling balls. Shit is about to hit the proverbial fan and Al'Kallach is ready to bring the pain.

Then Jane clasps both of them on their shoulders. "Now remember, sisters, what the therapist said. We are a team. And though sometimes we might get angry, we must communicate before resorting to forms of violence. Because we love each other. Because no one and nothing should get between us. Even someone as handsome and as dashing as Elias." She reaches forward with her hand. "Three Sisters forever." Begrudgingly, Al'Kallach and Ma'Ga'Ta lay their hands on hers. "On three now. One. Two. Three." All of their voices chime in together. "Three Sisters forever! Woo!"

What the...

They turn to me. "I'm hungry," says Ma'Ga'Ta.

"Temperature's just right," says Al'Kallach as she puts her finger in the boiling water.

"Let's talk over dinner," agrees Jane.

Now, wait. Wait a second. That's not how this was supposed to go. "Please good ladies, please don't boil me alive. I don't taste good, I swear. Much too gamy I've been told."

They grab the beam and start to lower it.

On second thought.

Children and sensitive souls may want to skip the page.

* * *

WHAT? Still here. Well… don't say I didn't warn you.

* * *

THE CRONES lower me into the pot, boil me alive, and enjoy a nice dinner. No joke. But they didn't account for one thing.

My gift.

I call it renewal.

And it's one badass skill. Or talent, really, since I did nothing to learn it. But that's a story for another time. Right now, all you need to concern yourself with is renewal lets me… well… renew.

Or revive. Or resurrect. You get the picture.

I always regenerate my body though, so here I stand, leaning against the doorway, watching as the Three Sisters devour the Iris special, aka my old corpse, aka disgusting.

I'll leave them to it. Because again, I'm not here for them. I'm here for Elias. And though the crones may be dimwitted, they are dangerous in a fight. It's why I let myself be captured—to extract information from them. Trying to beat it out of them would have been quite the hassle and not guaranteed to succeed, so I'll stay my blade for now. Old Uncle Sly would be proud. Brains before brawn, he always says. Though he says some weird shit too, so I probably shouldn't pat myself on the back quite yet. At any rate, it's time to go.

I wander down the stone hallway. More of a cave, really. A tunnel? Yeah, a damp and dark tunnel filled with buzzing flies and other creepy crawlies. Something squishes under my black leather boots making a wet sucking sound. It may only be mud, but it also may be a decomposing corpse, so let's not think too much about it.

So walking… walking… oh, what do we have here? A festival. A party. It appears the local monsters got together for a little fun in the crones' basement. A giant cave full of torches and natural light from the open ceiling. Dozens of bodies writhing to a chorus of beating drums. There are ghouls. And gargoyles. Their dancing is hard to watch, so I'll spare you the details. A satyr glances at me and winks, then leaps away on his goat legs to join the nymphs grinding in the corner. No one else gives me a second look. No one notices me and thinks, "Oh shit, run, badass hunter over here."

Why's that, Iris, you may be asking.

Because, little bird, I'm a monster too.

Well, half-monster. But we'll discuss that later.

The important thing is, I look human. Like a twenty-one-year-old woman, some would say. But there are monsters that appear pretty human. Succubus, for example. All they need to do is cover up their hairy legs and their little horns and they could pass for a cover model. So, as my legs are covered in black leather and my head is hidden under a black hood—noticing a trend yet?—I look enough a Succubus. Perhaps a shade not pretty enough, but I make up for it with a great personality. Yay!

Sorry...

I grew up with a Succubus. Dating was... difficult... when everyone was supernaturally and heck, naturally, attracted to your best friend. Still have some hard feelings about that. I should probably tell my therapist. If I had one...

Note: get a therapist who specializes in paranormal teenage angst.

Now that's handled, time to party. I groove my way to the nymphs and casually bring up that I'm trying to find Jane. Perchance she's in her room? Oh yeah. Where is it? Upstairs, take the third right. Thank you, creepy satyr.

I follow his directions and reach a dreary corridor that could really use some re-decorating. Seriously, why hang a picture of Captain America next to a picture of Dracula? It's... odd. Anyway, I'm alone here, the music from downstairs a barely audible thud reverberating through the floor. I draw my trusty twin daggers and step forward, a small part of my mind worried for the battle that is to come.

Then *he* shows up.

The destroyer of worlds. The butcher of armies. The Prince of—

Oh, it's only Imenath. Sorry, I thought it was actually someone dangerous.

"We meet again," growls Imenath, stepping forward from the shadows behind me, his entire body covered in silver armor resembling a skeleton. His head masked behind a helmet sprouting horns. He swings his giant spiked mace from his shoulders and grips it with both hands. "Will the hunter prevail—"

"Yep," I say.

"Or will Imenath the Terrible, number three on the most wanted list—"

"You're not number three anymore, buddy. You're not even on the list."

"Or," he continues, "will Imenath the Terrible have his revenge."

"Nope."

"Imenath will destroy you, lying hunter."

I sigh. This is so messing with my cover. "Hey, Imenath, buddy, remember that time when I captured you? You went to prison? Served your time? Got out early for good behavior?" I pat him on the shoulder. "You're not a criminal anymore. I'm not after you."

"I stole a chocolate bar from downstairs." He growls. "I am a menace to society. I am—"

"Great. Maybe the chocolate police will come after you. I don't know. Not my jurisdiction." I lean in conspiratorially. "But listen, I'm kinda here on a mission, you see. High-level stuff. I need to stay on the down low. And you're giving me away, man. I just, I just need some help here."

"Imenath will destroy puny hunter!" roars Imenath. He swings his giant mace with all his might at my head. To some, like Imenath himself, perhaps this would be a fierce and swift blow. But to me, well, it's as if he's moving in slow motion.

Oh boy. This is so embarrassing. I assumed I was past fighting level four monsters, but it seems some never learn. Well, I guess there's nothing left to do except...

I punch him in the face. He flies ten feet through the air, crashing through a window down the hall, falling, his voice echoing on the wind. "I will return..."

Now that's handled, back to the mission. Where was I? Oh yeah, about to break into Jane's room and capture Elias.

And again, sorry about that interruption. Imenath and I go way back. He used to be my mark when I was still figuring out how to break out as a hunter, make my own way and all that. He was my first real challenge, real wall, as it were in gamer speak, and it took about a year before I finally captured him. We had some good battles, Imenath and I, but what can I say except... some of us improved in life, some didn't. Imenath went to prison, I continued hunting, until I became number one in all the worlds. That's right. Iris, your girl, is the number one paranormal hunter of all time.

But even I have a final challenge.

And as I step into the crone's room and hide behind a stone chair, there he is.

Elias.

FULL NAME: Elias Vane Spero

Classification: Half Vampire / Half Fae

Title: High Prince of Hell

Physical Description: Six feet tall, all muscle, black tattoos, dark hair, blue eyes

Number one on the most wanted list

Wanted alive for all manner of nefarious deeds

HE IS the most dangerous man in the world. And he's standing ten feet in front of me. Bastard better be ready.

Because I'm coming for him.

ELIAS

I watch from cover, studying the cavern, planning my attack. It's a large space with rounded walls that curve up, revealing an open ceiling in the center. Beneath the opening is a bed carved from a boulder and covered in furs. I'm describing it in a way that might sound charming. But really, little bird, it's drafty, dirty, and kinda gross. There are bugs. Those furs look flea-infested. And who wants to sleep on a stone bed under the stars on nights when it's pouring rain? Or really, any night. Talk about backbreaking. But hey, to each their own.

Elias stands on a patch of moss-covered stone near the bed. Beams of moonlight dance on his pale skin, his dark hair drifting in the light wind. He's shirtless, for reasons I'd rather not imagine... (Crap, it's too late. Now I'm mentally seeing him and Jane doing the horizontal tango and it is nasty, get it out. Note to self: Gouge out third eye.) So back to the half-naked vampire who's only wearing black pants and black boots as he strides across the cave in three easy steps. I'm pretty certain I'm just imagining it, but the very earth seems to quake under his feet. As if Mother Nature herself doesn't want to get in his way.

He's right in front of me, but he can't see me as I crouch behind the chair and palm my daggers. I need to strike but...

Something pulls me toward him. Draws me closer. They say Elias picked up some tricks from his uncle, the Prince of Lust, and I can't discount that theory. His movements are both graceful and strong. His smile both inviting and dangerous. His eyes both piercing and seductive. If one wasn't afraid of sounding cheesy, they might call him dreamy, yummy...

Wait a second... what's happening? Oh no, my legs feel like jelly. Crap, my palms are sweaty, my heart beating faster. What's going on? I want to leap out of my hiding place and yell, "take me," but I shouldn't... I mean, I shouldn't, right?

Snap out of it, Iris. It's just some unnatural power making you hot and heavy. It's not real. Get it together. It's hunting time.

The magical pull fades away—with some serious force of will on my part—and my focus returns. Elias may have eluded me before, (twenty-one times exactly, but who's counting?) but today... I'm gonna catch the bitch.

I wait for him to turn his back to me, and sure enough he does, revealing the coils of serpentine black tattoos across his muscled body. He walks over to the rumpled bed in the corner, clearly disheveled from a night of passion, and grabs a silver pitcher from the side table, then pours himself a cup of something red and sips the viscous liquid, staining his pale lips a dark crimson.

His weapons—a sword and dagger—lie casually against the side of the bed. They are two steps away from their master, far enough to give me the upper hand. I palm my—

"You can come out," Elias says, his voice dark and smooth like a glass of rich wine.

I groan. How does he always do that? Reluctantly, I leave my hiding place, daggers raised. "You have nowhere to run this time," I say.

He chuckles so charismatically it's almost disarming. "My dear Iris, you should know by now, I have no intention of running. Your company is so pleasant, after all." He puts the cup of blood down and walks up to a painting of... well, one ugly ass crone, who I can only presume was Jane's mother, and pulls it open like a door, revealing a safe carved within the stone wall. In an instant, he spins the dial, imputing the proper combination and unlocking the container. "Ah," he says, eyes glinting. "Finally." He reaches within the safe and draws out a sword, more beautiful and deadly than any I have ever seen. Ancient glyphs engrave the steel, glimmering in the light. The air itself stirs around the weapon, and as Elias sweeps the blade before him, it seems to sing a haunting melody on the wind. "The Moonlight Sword," Elias says softly, as if speaking to a lover.

"So, that's why you came here."

"Yes, though Jane's company was pleasurable as well." He glances at the bed with a smirk, and I shiver as unwanted images once again fill my mind. (My third eye gauging trick didn't work, little bird.) Elias shakes his head. "So human of you," he continues. "There is beauty in all things, Iris. Perhaps one day you will understand. Even a crone can be a maiden."

His words pour so smoothly from his lips, so easy to believe. But he's a liar. A trickster. "You used her," I say. "To get the combination. Now you steal from her."

He walks back to the bed and takes another sip of blood from his bronze cup. "I prefer to think of it as an arrangement. Both parties benefited."

He's talking too much. Stalling. Time to end this. "Elias Vane Spero, lay down your arms and surrender yourself to the First Hunter."

He ignores me, studying the sword in his grasp. "This blade was stolen from my father years ago," Elias says. "All my life I have searched for it. I will not give it away now. For my father—"

"Your father is ashamed of you," I spit. "Fenris Vane, King of all vampires, who brought peace to his kind, raised a son who steals and kills and makes a mockery of his name."

Elias's eyes turn dark. When he speaks, it is a roar that shakes the very room. "You know nothing of my family. You know nothing of me."

He is angry. Good. It will dull his senses, make him weaker.

"Leave now, Iris," he says. "You cannot defeat the Moonlight

Sword. The steel is indestructible. The craftsmanship unfathomable. The sword was forged in—"

I leap forward, striking with my twin daggers as he monologues.

Elias reacts in an instant, bringing his blade up to meet my own. Steel clashes. Sparks fly.

And the Moonlight Sword breaks in two.

The top half falls, crumbling into dust.

"Oh," says Elias, raising an eyebrow. "Well, I didn't expect that to happen."

We stand frozen, only inches apart. "Perhaps it was old," I say.

"Old?" He winces. "Old? The Moonlight Sword doesn't get old. It's a bloody fake."

I shrug, because like, seriously, I do not care. Then I strike again.

He leaps out of the way, landing in a roll, and jumping back to his feet next to the bed, grabbing his sword and dagger. He draws his weapons from their sheaths and swings them elegantly through the air. "Just like last time, then."

He lunges.

I parry. "You may have escaped me before—"

"Twenty one times, to be exact," he shrugs, "but who's counting?"

I literally snarl as I strike back, spit flying from my mouth.

"Eww. That's disgusting," Elias parries my blows as he retreats backwards, avoiding the flying phlegm. "Is this a new tactic? I must say, it's working."

He spins past me, his dagger slicing the tip of my shoulder. The cut hurts my pride more than my body.

"You're sloppy today," says Elias. "Was it something you ate? A tummy ache?"

My dagger catches his forearm, drawing blood. "I'm feeling fine, thank you very much." I strike again, tearing a hole in his pants.

"Now, now, Iris," teases Elias. "I didn't think we were at that stage of our relationship. But if you're willing—"

I knock the dagger out of his hand, leaving him with only a sword. "I don't date criminals," I say.

He smirks. "Who said anything about dating?"

We exchange blows. Both of us a bit clumsier than before. Our palms are now covered in sweat. Our breathing becomes more labored. We groan and roar as we battle.

Elias cuts a thin streak across my neck, drawing a scarlet line. He sniffs the air vigorously. "Intoxicating as ever, Iris. What I would give for a drop of that blood…"

I raise an eyebrow as I parry. "Would you surrender?"

"Perhaps."

"Too bad I'm about to catch you anyway."

He chuckles, his laugh marvelous, as he cuts me lightly across the thigh. He lands a kick to my knee, pushing me back. Not good. Being half human, I'm tiring out before him. I need something to shift the balance.

But Iris, you have renewal. Even if he kills you, you'll come back!

Not quite, little bird.

Renewal only works once a day.

That's the deal with greater gifts. They need to recharge, as it were.

I know, I know, what you're thinking. Iris, why did you let the crones boil you alive then? Well… it's not like I intended to be a late night snack. I thought I'd talk my way out of it, or at least break through the chains, but no… they just happened to have trimantium— nearly unbreakable steel that is—on hand, and of course they also just happened to have started therapy.

Then Iris, why didn't you simply cancel the mission?

Because, little bird, that is not an option. I've been tracking Elias for months this time around, and there is no way I'm coming home empty-handed for the twenty-second time.

I thrust my daggers forward and leap into the air, howling like a banshee. The move catches Elias off guard as I hoped, and he stumbles backwards, knocking into the bedpost. I land on top of him, blades aimed straight for his heart, but he drops his sword and grabs my wrists as we tumble on to the mattress, fighting amongst the furs. I pin him down with my knees as I take jabs at his head.

Elias frowns, avoiding my blows. "I generally prefer to be on top, but I suppose we can make an exception for the first time—"

I stab a pillow instead of his face, and feathers fly into my mouth. I thrust again and—cough, cough, oh these feathers are horrible, some are even still bloody from whatever foul beast they were plucked from —we fall out of the bed, and he knocks away my daggers with his fists. Unarmed, we begin to wrestle on the stone floor, trying to lock each other in a hold. I grab his leg. He yanks my arm.

I reach forward. He kicks me back.

I strike at his jaw. He leans away.

"And so it goes," says Elias, rolling in front of the fireplace. "You fight. I flirt. It always ends the same way."

A primitive growl escapes my throat. "No. This time, I will bring you in."

"Dum spiro spero," he says, glancing at the broken sword on the ground, as if he looks at a pile of shattered dreams.

"Dum spiro what now?" I ask, using the moment to catch my breath.

"Dum spiro spero. While I breathe, I hope." He sighs. "It's something my mother would always say."

"I wonder if she still hopes for you," I say bitterly.

He smiles, though there is no joy in it. "What is the bounty on me now? Five million? Ten?"

"Actually, it's um… fifty thousand."

"Fifty? Only fifty thousand… what the… listen, you tell your bosses that's not gonna cut it."

"I don't do it for the money," I say.

"By the Spirits," he says, shaking his head. "Please don't tell me you do it for justice?"

I say nothing.

He laughs. "Have you ever wondered who makes the most wanted list?"

"The Council of Hunters—"

"The council," he says, nodding. "Ever looked into their members? The enemies they make? The money they exchange?"

My hands sweat, and not just from fighting anymore. "What do you mean?"

"I mean, it's not all black and white, dear Iris. I mean…" He pauses, his next words so soft I can barely make them out. "Lix Tetrax."

"Lix what now?"

"Ask your boss about it sometime." He stands, cracking his knuckles. "Now, I hate to cut things short, my dear, but I have somewhere to be soon, so can we wrap this up, please? Leave some unfulfilled passion for next time?"

"Sure. Once you surrender."

He scoffs.

That's it. Enough talking. Time to shift the tide. Time to use my secret weapon.

I reach behind me and pull a canister from the back of my belt.

Elias's eyes go wide. "Is that a…"

"A freaking bomb? You bet your ass it is."

I toss the explosive at him. He dodges, but of course, I expected that, and the canister lands right where I wanted. Inside the fireplace.

The bomb explodes.

The cavern trembles.

And the ceiling collapses into hundreds of rocks.

Elias looks up. "Oh, fu—"

THE WHITE RIDER

I may or may not be stuck under some rocks. Don't judge me.

"What a lovely idea this was," groans Elias.

He's judging me. I see it in his gorgeous eyes. But what do I care, he's trapped under a mountain of stone. Only his head is popping out free, and it's time I played whack the vampire. Except... oh right, I'm trapped too.

"Eghh... Aghh... errr..."

"Why are you making those noises?" I ask.

Elias clenches his jaw, the vein on his neck ready to explode. "I'm trying... eghh... to... errr... break free. You?"

"I'm perfectly comfortable." In reality, I'm taking a break. In a moment, I'll be able to push these rocks off me and... I smirk, glancing up at the ceiling... or well, what used to be the ceiling. It was slightly open before, but now it's truly blown away. Get it? Blown away? Because the bomb... Oh, come on, you're no fun...

Anyway, there's only the night sky above us. Perfect.

I purse my lips and whistle. A clear bright sound, so loud it echoes through the caverns below. Bet you're gonna try that at home now.

"Calling for backup?" asks Elias.

"Composing a new song." I whistle an improvised tune. Quite haunting and brilliant, if I do say so myself. Someone should be recording, seriously. Grammys here I come.

"What did you mean?" I ask. "Lix Tetrax?"

He pauses. "I…"

My haunting whistle drifts through the air. Problem is, I'm not whistling anymore. What the…

The eerie tune keeps playing, and a chill creeps up on me, sinking into my bones. A layer of frost crawls over the stone, clinging to my skin like a moist film—which is totally as gross as it sounds, in case you were wondering. The specks of flame from the fireplace, still burning, shimmer and turn silver, the warmth dying. And then there's a song… a song of children singing on the wind.

Now, I know what you're thinking. Children singing on the wind? I must be messing with you. And maybe I am, a smidgen. But not about this.

A choir of young voices echoes around me as the wind begins to howl. And the song they sing is thus…

He'll come in the night
In armor of white
Riding a steed of snow

Three signs there are
That mean he's not far
Silver army in tow

First comes the frost
Second the flame

Third are the voices
of those he has slain

"HE'S HERE," mutters Elias, his voice devoid of the confidence it possessed a moment ago. His eyes dart back and forth around the cavern, and for the first time, I see him afraid.

"You need to leave," he continues. "Now."

I gather my strength and push one of my hands out from below the rocks. It'll take a while to free the rest of my body. "Good try, but I'm not leaving without my bounty."

"Then you better start digging me up." He struggles against the mountain of stone, but he's not strong enough, or perhaps not well-rested enough. It's not because the pile on top of him is about three times the size of the pile on top of me. No. That couldn't be it at all.

I free my second arm and start digging out my torso. "So how are you doing this? Hidden blue tooth speaker? Lighting effects on the flame?"

"This isn't me."

"So what... the DJ put on a nursery rhyme downstairs?" I chuckle, and it's totally not the most awkward-I'm-going-to-piss-my-pants chuckle ever. Nope. Total confidence. Even though... I know I'm wrong. Elias can't do this. The thing is... No one can.

"You're not the only one after me," he says.

I scoff, my body finally free, as I get to work on my legs. "Well... duh, every hunter wants to be the one to catch you, though few dare to try."

Elias shakes his head, staring into the distance, into the darkness in the corner of the cavern, where the shadows seem to coalesce and bleed. "This isn't a hunter," he whispers. "It's the White Rider."

Thud.

Thud.

Thud.

Footsteps. They come from the darkness. Drawing near.

Thud.

Thud.

Thud.

The sound of hooves clacking on icy stone.

And then I see him.

The White Rider.

He comes from the shadows. He comes from nothing. Riding a steed the color of snow, the blanket covering his horse torn and ragged and gray. He dismounts, his landing shaking the very earth, the ground beneath his feet turning to ice. White armor hangs off his massive body, twisting around his limbs like roots grown wild. A helmet with horns, though perhaps they are more like branches drifting in the wind, and a crown of spikes adorn his head. His breath fogs the air, though I cannot see his mouth. It is covered completely in white.

As he walks, he drags his sword behind him, a massive thing of silver steel, scraping the ground, a sound that tears at my mind. When he speaks, his voice is low and unnatural, like stone sliding over gravel. But there is something else as well. A second voice layered over the first. A whisper I can barely hear.

"Elias," says the White Rider. "My dear Elias. The time has come."

"You will not take me," says Elias, jaw clenched, eyes fierce.

The rider looks over the mountain of rocks, silver eyes shining in the moonlight. "I don't believe you have a choice, old friend." His eyes stop, settling on me. "Iris…"

"You know who I am?" I ask, only my left foot trapped now.

"Everyone knows who you are, First Hunter." His last words are a whisper, echoing in my mind.

"I've heard of you, too," I say, trying to keep this thing, whatever it is, talking. "But as a story. A tale meant to scare children."

He chuckles, a deep sound, as if the earth were shifting down below. "Do I look like a story, Iris?"

I say nothing. I just meet his eyes. And I don't break my stare.

He turns, focusing once again on the vampire. "I suppose I should thank you, Iris, for catching my prey for me." He bends down on one knee, and with a long white finger, he lifts Elias's chin so they are face to face. "Come willingly, and I will allow the girl to live. Struggle, and you will watch as both fire and ice consume her body, and listen as her screams echo through the night."

"Think you may have the wrong person," I say, frowning. "Elias doesn't care for anyone."

The White Rider just chuckles, turning back to his prey. "So what will it be, old friend?"

Elias glances at me, then back at the rider. And in that moment, something changes, and the spark that drove Elias Vane Spero dies. "I… " he begins, voice low and broken, his head down. "I—"

A roar fills the air. Like a clap of thunder from above.

The rider and Elias look up. But not me. I don't have to. Because my backup is finally here. I mean, you and I both know I wasn't actually whistling just for fun, right?

"Theo!" I yell.

And my silver lion descends from the sky, white wings unfurled and spanning the cavern. He soars down at the White Rider, claws shining in the pale light of the moon.

The armored creature jumps away at the last moment, much more agile than its steel shell would indicate, and my lion lands between us, as tall as two grown men, roaring at the one who threatened me.

"A manticore," says the rider, admiring my mighty Theo. "I wonder, how did you tame such a marvelous beast?"

I pull my foot free, finally escaping the rocks, and leap to Theo's side, standing by his silver mane as his tail whips around me, my daggers drawn and ready. "How about you come closer and I tell you."

The rider flicks his sword up, clasping it in both hands. The blade is thick, double-edged and runs the length of my body. How he can be both so fast and so strong is the real mystery here.

"You cannot fight him," yells Elias.

I beg to differ.

I wink at Theo, my silver manticore, and—

Yelling comes from beyond the door. The sound of a dozen footsteps. Seems the monsters finally realized someone blew up the ceiling. Took them long enough.

The White Rider looks to the door, then back at me. "Perhaps another time, Iris." He leaps onto his massive steed, and before I can follow, he rides back into the shadow.

I run after him, nearly slipping on the ice, swinging my daggers, but I hit only a stone wall in the darkness. There is no door. No window. And yet he is gone.

"Guess we scared him off," I say, putting away my daggers.

Theo grunts in approval, shaking his silver mane.

"No," says Elias, looking around. "He must have sensed something… or someone."

I raise an eyebrow. "The drunk monsters downstairs? Pretty sure none of them are higher than level five."

"No. Someone powerful is coming."

The door to the room bursts open and dozens of angry monsters begin to file in. The nymphs are pissed. The satyr found a spiked club somewhere. The three crones carry butcher knives and, upon seeing me alive, are understandably quite confused. Jane notices her room, specifically the lack of ceiling, then Elias trapped under a pile of rocks, and faints. A few of the goblins seem deterred by my manticore, but most are unconcerned. This might be problem.

Theo growls, ready to protect me with his life.

"Easy boy," I whisper, petting his silver fur. Most of these monsters are innocent. I can't get into a fight with them.

"Hey," says Elias, smiling. "Al'Kallach. Ma'Ga'Ta. I didn't know you two were here. How about giving your friend a hand?"

They both cross their arms like crones scorned.

"Shouldn't have slept with their sister," I say quietly.

He shakes his head. "Come now. There's enough of me to go around."

They don't budge.

He chuckles nervously, his head bopping up and down from the rocks. He points at me with a free finger. "Let me remind you, she invaded your home. I was a welcome guest, and… wait a moment, why does your manticore look like it wants to eat me?"

I smirk. "Theo doesn't like when people speak ill of me."

Theo bares his teeth, crouching low.

The nervous chuckle continues. "Now, now, Theo. I didn't mean it…" He turns his head back to the monsters, speaking rapidly. "Trust me, I didn't cause this mess. She's the one who brought the bomb."

"Bomb?" the word spreads through the crowd like a contagious yawn.

Okay, this definitely might be a problem.

I reach into my cloak and pull out my hunter badge, flashing it for the crowd. "Official business here. Nothing to worry about. Everyone please go back to your party."

"A hunter!" says the satyr, spitting toward me. "A hunter put my brother away for life."

On second thought, the badge may not have been such a good idea.

I grit my teeth at Elias, manticore style, really wishing I could break my personal code just this once and kill him.

He seems to shrug under the stone, then turns back toward the monsters. "She's not just a hunter," says Elias, nodding. "She's the First Hunter. The best. She probably put all your relatives away."

The crowd glares as one. I swear I hear someone sharpening a knife.

"So how about it," continues Elias, "you help a fellow monster out and… wait a second, what are you doing, Iris?"

Enough talking Elias. I grab a rock and smash him in the skull so hard the stone shatters. He falls unconscious, head limp and dangling.

"She killed him!" roars the satyr.

Shit.

They begin to march forward, the—

"Stop," a female voice yells from behind.

They pause, parting like water, as a monster in a brown cloak steps forward, her legs covered in a dark auburn fur, and gestures for everyone to go quiet. They do, watching her for more orders, and I wonder, for a moment, if this is the monster the White Rider sensed.

She pulls off her hood, revealing lavish red hair and two horns that are just too cute. Her lips are plump and the perfect shade of red. Her eyes are like chocolate. The satyr, upon seeing her, literally starts to salivate. She is, I will admit, the hottest succubus ever born.

Thank the gods she's also my best friend.

CALLIE

The succubus turns to the crowd. "She's with me, everyone." I can see her power sweep over them in the way they start to blush, to drool, to stare, each of them mesmerized by her every word. "Now, why don't we get this party back on track. Satyr."

He hops up and down with joy at being singled out. "Yes, beautiful goddess?"

She stares at him seductively. "I need a big, hairy man like you to go downstairs and turn the music back on twice as loud as before. Can you do that for me? Please?"

His tongue wags out of his mouth as he nods, before he turns and rushes out the door.

The succubus eyes the crowd. "Why don't you all join him?" They nod enthusiastically and start to file out, casting sad glances over their shoulders. "I'll be down in a moment, loves. Soon as I catch up with my bestie over here."

Their faces fill with cheer, heartened by the prospect of seeing the succubus again. Her name's Callie, by the way. Callie Lavish. If I were to rate her level—and I don't usually rate friends, by the way—I'd rate her a level nine. You just saw why. Perhaps the White Rider wannabe feared taking both of us on. Who can say at this point?

She turns to me, an impatient expression on her face as she waits for the monsters to leave. Once they are all gone, she squeals. "O.M.G. You got him. I can't believe you got him!"

I smile smugly. "Who's the best hunter in the world?"

"Ah, you are." We high five, and perform our secret handshake—which I will not explain to you, because… duh, secret—after which she turns her attention to Theo, gently bumping her head against his. "Who's a good boy? Who's a good boy? Did you help your Mama capture the big bad guy? Huh? I bet you did. Yes."

The silver lion purrs in response, nudging his cheeks against her little brown horns. Callie giggles, rubbing him under his chin until he falls over on his back, demanding petting from us both.

"You did good, yes," I say, scratching him behind the ear in his favorite spot. "Yeah, you did."

He closes his eyes in happiness.

Callie grins, pulling back. She walks over to Elias and squats down on her goat legs, studying him up close, pinching his cheeks with her manicured nails. "He's even more handsome than in the photos."

I shrug, moving to pet Theo's belly. "Eh, he's okay for a vampire."

"Well, this vampire can have me any day." She stands back up, rubbing her palms together. "He's so yummy I want to eat him. Or… " her eyes light up with mischief, "the other way around."

"Anyway…" I say, because I need to change the subject like right now. "How'd you know I could use your help?"

Callie shakes her head. "Oh, I didn't come here to help you."

"No?"

"I came because you were running late."

I scan my memory, pausing the belly rubs on my cat as I think. Theo licks my hands to remind them what to do. "Late for what now?"

She winces. "Oh, and don't be mad."

"Why would I be mad?"

She winces even more. "I called your uncle."

The petting stops. I simmer, anger boiling up inside me. "Are you fu—"

"What a bloody mess," says Uncle Sly, appearing out of thin air before us, dressed in a perfectly tailored black tuxedo. He wipes his brow with a purple silk kerchief and raises a bushy gray eyebrow in my direction. "What do I always say? Containment, people. Containment."

I gesture at Elias. "He seems pretty contained to me."

Sly sighs so loudly you'd think he was doing vocal exercises. "How many people saw you here, hmm? How much destruction of property occurred?" He pauses. Then leans in and kisses me on both of my cheeks. "By the way, I'm so proud of you, darling. So proud."

"Thanks... and about four dozen monsters saw me, I guess, and I blew up the ceiling?"

"Are you not sure?"

I squint. "Well... it's kinda turning hazy."

He sighs again. "At least you finally caught the bloody bastard." He shakes his head disapprovingly at Elias. "His parents are good people. They must be so ashamed. So ashamed." He turns back to me, grasping my shoulders. "There's no challenging you now. You're the First Hunter, no doubt about that."

"Thanks, Uncle Sly."

He glances up at the sky. "We better get him out of here before the sun comes up. Besides, you have somewhere to be."

"Right," I say thoughtfully. "That thing Callie and I were just talking about." I look at her, my eyes pleading, because I can so not remember the thing.

Sly huffs. "You forgot, didn't you? You always forget." He pauses, rubbing his brow again, mumbling. "This is a disaster. You're going to be late again."

"Where?"

"Why, the masquerade ball, of course."

"Oh shit." I start to pull rocks off Elias, tossing them over my shoulder in a frenzy. "That's tonight?"

"In an hour," says Callie.

Of course it is. Right in the middle of the night, partly for dramatic effect, but mostly so the vampires can attend.

"And you still need to ready yourself," adds Sly. "In hopes we can perhaps finally find you... a suitable match."

"He means to say you need to get laid," adds Callie.

"So crass," says Sly, wincing in disgust. "But yes, that's what I meant."

A rock almost hits him in the head, totally by accident. "I don't need my uncle and best friend to set me up."

"We're worried about you, darling," says Sly delicately. "About your social life."

"About the fact you don't have one," adds Callie.

I groan, and totally not in a sullen I'm-acting-like-a-teenager kind of way. "I'm going to the ball for one reason and one reason only. To impress the Council of Hunters so they promote me to watcher and eventually give me a seat on the council as a keeper."

"But then..." Callie's eyes light up. "You'd be the youngest watcher ever."

I pull off another rock, not looking at my friend or uncle. "Exactly."

Sly sighs again, as if he's going for a record. "Which is why they will never select you. You're too—"

"Young, I know," I finish. "But I'm also the youngest person to make First Hunter. And now," I pull my mark out from under the rubble, grinning. "I've captured Elias Vane Spero. Number one on the most wanted list. They'll have to promote me."

But Iris, you might be thinking, you're the First Hunter, why would you want a promotion? Because, little bird, there are two main perks to being a watcher. First, I can order other hunters around. And second, and this is really the most important part, one needs to be a watcher to be considered for a seat on the council. My reasons for being on the council... well, we'll get to those later.

Sly says nothing for a while, simply looks at me, his eyes kind. "I hope you get it, darling. I really hope you do."

"Thanks, Uncle." I kiss him on the cheek, before dragging Elias over the stone floor and throwing him across Theo's back. I pull a pair a trimantium shackles (made of the strongest material we hunters possess) from my cloak and bind the vampire's wrists together. Once I'm sure he'll stay secured, I hop on top of Theo, holding onto his mane for control. "See you back at the Black Lotus."

"Wait," hollers Callie. "Can I catch a ride?"

"Sure," I say, my mind totally fixed on the present and not the masquerade ball.

She climbs on behind me, holding onto my waist. Damn, she smells good.

Sly waves goodbye. "See you two in a jiffy." He vanishes into thin air as quickly as he appeared. He's never told me how he does that, by the way. Just Sly being Sly, as usual.

I lightly tug on Theo's mane, and he spreads his massive wings, taking flight through the expanded skylight my bomb helped build. Really, they should be sending me a thank you note. This room needed a good renovation. Callie whoops loudly in my ear. "Oh, I forgot how much fun this is."

She's right. Sometimes I forget how lucky I am to fly. To twirl through the sky against the wind, the clouds rushing past me. To be one with the air. As we glide, Theo's fur shimmers a pale blue, taking on the colors of the night. It is a lesser gift of his, much like my gift of renewal. It lets him blend in with his surroundings. And it keeps the normals down below from seeing a giant flying lion and calling the cops.

For a moment, I am lost in a beautiful dream of moonbeams and stars and darkness.

Callie fidgets behind me. "Have you felt his muscles? I mean... wow."

"Seriously?"

"Just saying. This Elias, how sure are we he's guilty?"

"Let's see... he's wanted for theft, murder, indecent exposure—"

"But how sure are we he did all those things?"

I shrug. "I suppose the council will find out."

"Yeah, I suppose.... Oh, I think he's waking up."

"Here." I pull a small green vial from my cloak and hand it to her. "Let him inhale this."

She grabs it and places it under his nose. After a few whiffs, Elias is as limp as a giant worm being eaten by a sea serpent. It reminds me, I've caught my bounty, but there may be a bigger fish out there.

"Hey," I say quietly, "You heard anything about a White Rider imposter?"

Callie rests her chin on my shoulder. "Like the story? No. Why?"

I shrug casually, much more casually than I feel about the whole matter. "Just someone I ran into."

"Huh. You should ask Sly."

"Yeah, sure," I say in what is definitely not a sarcastic way.

She groans. "What's up with you two? Did you have a thing? You had a thing, didn't you?"

I sigh and... crap, it's like I'm becoming my uncle. "He doesn't think I should try for watcher. We had a fight before my hunt."

"But he said—"

"What he said and what he means are two very different things."

Callie nods, patting my shoulder gently. "That's Sly for you. Guess that's why you didn't like me calling him, huh? Well, he probably only wants to make sure you're ready."

"I'm the best hunter there is. How much more ready can I be?"

She shrugs. "Perhaps there are things you and I aren't privy to. About the watchers. And the council."

Her words remind me of something Elias said. But I can't dwell on that. He was trying to manipulate me, after all. I need a distraction, and fortunately, we're about to arrive.

Theo glides past the glimmering buildings below, until he hovers above a secluded forest. When he dives down at full speed, the wind lashes at my skin as we rush toward a thicket of overgrown trees. We're about to crash into the branches, when we break through the illusion, revealing an open valley of soft grass and calm water. Theo lands in a clearing by a stream glittering in the moonlight, where silver flowers grow by the bank. The Valley of Silence.

It's the place I was born. Or so I'm told.

Now it serves as my base of operations. Where I go to get away from the bureaucracy of the Council of Hunters.

I jump off the lion and untie Elias. "Help me carry him."

Callie nods, and together we move him toward a small cabin blowing smoke out the chimney. Next to it, three llamas graze within a confined wooden fence. They are called Wit, Smarts, and Brains, and no one but me can tell them apart. Well, no one but me and Theo. He jumps over the fence, playing with the llamas, and by playing, I mean mostly chasing them as they run away. They were a gift from Sly, back when I was little. Say what you want about llamas, but they are so undeniably cute and awesome (that's what you were going to say, right?) and they made me one happy birthday girl.

I kick open the door to the small cabin... Well, it looks like a small cabin from the outside. Inside, it sprawls out into a luscious manor with multiple rooms. A fire crackles by the entryway, smelling of pine and charcoal. Brazilian cherry hardwood lines the floor, the perfect shade of auburn. Tapestries depicting legendary monsters hang on the walls, handmade by the way. Welcome to my not so humble abode. My pride and joy. You should have seen it before I got my hands on it. It was gray and dusty and full of mold and spiders. But as I kept collecting bounties and improving at my craft, I used most of my earnings to polish the place. Now, years later, it's quite the marvel. My own little slice of paradise.

We drop Elias on the couch, and I rush to the closet, because I so do not know what to wear for the party.

"Nope," says Callie. "Not that one. Not that one. Nope. Not... ah, that is perfect."

I pull out my silver dress and start to pull off my current clothes. Callie doesn't stare, but she doesn't leave either. We're close that way, after once being trapped together by an ogre for two months. I'm about slip on the silver dress, when Callie slaps my hand, forcing me to drop it.

"What the hell?"

Callie looks at me with a raised eyebrow. "You smell like monster ass. You're covered in dust and rubble and blood. You need to bathe, my dear."

Oh. Right. Forgot about that in all the rush. I ask Callie to keep an eye on Elias, which she is a little too happy about, while I take the world's fastest shower. Getting my hair dry is another matter, but fortunately, I have a magical trick for that. Sorry, can't tell you about it. Patent pending and all. If I told you, I'd have to kill you. You know how it is.

Callie nods approvingly when I return, and finally lets me don the silver dress. It hugs my body tightly, revealing my bare shoulders. I look around for the matching white gloves and find them under a pair of hunting boots. Callie dangles a pair of heels in front of me, but I slip on a pair of flats instead. I require the maneuverability, what can I say? Now I just need... "Crap. I forgot the mask."

Callie smiles coyly and pulls something from her coat. She holds up a silver mask covered in iridescent crystals. "Got you covered, bestie."

I take the mask and hug my dearest friend. "Thank you."

Checking myself out in the mirror, I must admit, I am looking fine. Once my mask is secured around my face, Callie nods approvingly.

"No one will be able to keep their eyes off you," says the succubus, which means she's probably right.

"I need them to see me as more than a hunter," I say, applying a shade of red lipstick. "They need to see that I can represent the council with dignity. Even during important social occasions."

"And they will," says Callie, grabbing the lipstick from me. "Now let's go."

"Right—"

"Well, don't you look lovely," comes a sultry voice from the couch. Elias. How is he already awake?

He sits up, his eyes admiring.

Callie and I exchange a look, a signal only besties recognize, and she walks forward, pouting her lips at Elias, palming the green sleeping potion behind her back. "Hey baby. How about you and I have a little cuddle, huh?"

In an instant he stands, spinning past her and grabbing the vial from her before she even knows what happened. He tosses it over his shoulder and out a window without looking. "Sorry love, but your charms won't work on me," he says gently. The air between us seems to shimmer with tension as he steps toward me, his eyes fixed on mine. "Seems you caught me, Iris. So what are you going to do with me?"

His words and tone are laced with subtext that make parts of my body flush with heat, but I ignore those feelings and straighten my back, trying to match him in height, mostly succeeding. "Who's the White Rider wannabe?"

His voice is low. "The less you know, the better, trust me."

"Protecting a fellow criminal?"

He eyes me up and down. "Protecting someone."

Callie steps between us, and it's only then I realize how close Elias and I are, our lips almost touching. "We need to go," says the succubus. "The party's about to start."

Elias grins. "Am I invited?"

I scoff and brush past him, taking off my necklace, a black iron key, and walk toward the front door. "Once we're at the Lotus, behave, or I'll knock you out again."

"Sounds fun." His smirk turns to a frown. "But I thought there was no violence allowed at the hotel?"

"The rules don't apply to criminals who try to flee."

"What if it's less trying... and more succeeding?"

I shake my head, standing at the cabin door with my necklace, a childhood keepsake Sly enchanted with whatever magicks he keeps hidden. I put it into the lock, any lock will work. And turn. When I open the door, the way doesn't lead to the valley, but instead into a lavish hotel. The Black Lotus.

Now...

I know you've heard about this next part. Read about it, at least. The incident, as most like to call it. You're wondering, were Iris and Elias both in on it? Did they work together? That is, after all, why you're reading this, right? To find out. I can assure you, it's much more complicated than that.

THE BLACK LOTUS

J walk in like a boss.

The hottest succubus in the world to my left. The Prince of Darkness to my right. If I could move in slow motion right now, I would. Let's just pretend I am.

Now let me set the scene...

The halls are pretty empty right now, no doubt because of the party, so that leaves us three alone for the moment. A red carpet unfurls beneath us, like movie star style except more grand. Everything else—walls, ceiling, floor—is pure white marble carved in ancient Greece during the reign of Alexander the Great himself. (Totally legit story, by the way.) Up above, dazzling crystal chandeliers cover everything in a warm golden hue like sweet, sweet honey, and red doors line the hallways, hiding lavish rooms home to all manner of monsters.

Temporary homes for most, of course, since the Black Lotus is, in the end, a hotel. A safe haven for those who don't belong elsewhere. Perhaps that is why I was left here as a baby.

Alone.

Abandoned.

:(

Ah, it wasn't that bad. I grew up in a freakin' paranormal hotel, after all, learning from all sorts of guests and wanderers. All under the careful eye of Uncle Sly. And now I return home triumphant. And look, a group has already gathered down the hall, waiting for the grand golden doors to open and the masquerade ball to commence. When they see me, their eyes light up and—

"Elias! O.M.G. it's him. I can't believe it's him." She actually says O.M.G. As in the letters.

They almost trample each other to reach the prince. They even ignore Callie—which is really saying something.

"Will you sign my invitation?"

"Sign my arm."

"Sign my boobs!" says a young Fae woman with pointed ears decorated with green emerald earrings to match her dress. And yes, in case you were wondering, she actually does pull said dress open to give my mark access to... well, everything.

Elias chuckles warmly. "Ladies and gentlemen, don't fret, there's enough Elias to go around." He glances at me. "Iris, do you have a pen?"

I grab him by the ear and pull him past the crowd.

"Now, now, that's not necessary, love," Elias say, wincing. "I haven't—"

A shriek.

Behind us.

I turn and see the young Fae woman who bared her chest to him a moment ago rush towards us, dagger in hand. "Elias, I will save you!" she yells. "Then we can be together forever."

Elias raises an eyebrow. I just sigh. The cray-cray is in full force today.

I'm about to try and talk her down when she focuses her attention on me. "And you. You hussy. You will never have him. I will gut you and feed you to dogs before I let you lay another finger on what is mine."

She raises her dagger and...

Snap.

Her knees collapse, and she falls to the red carpet, dropping the dagger, limbs twisting at odd angles. "No, please. Please," she pleads.

Snap.

Her voice goes quiet. Her mouth moves but she makes no sounds.

Snap.

She freezes. Still as a mangled statue.

Sly walks out from around the corner, his fingers held up, ready to snap once more. "Seems someone forgot the rules," he says, towering over the Fae woman in his perfect black tux. "No violence at the Black Lotus. And against my niece, no less. Tsk, tsk." He glances at me to make sure I'm okay before returning his attention to the Fae.

Her eyes are red, begging for mercy.

Sly tilts his head, frowning compassionately. "Now, since all harm was prevented, I suppose I can be lenient. Perhaps ten years in the dungeon shall do." He snaps his fingers once more, and two people emerge from the crowd, dressed as fancy as everyone else but completely in black. I recognize their faces. Bobby and Poppy. Two of the best Fixers at the hotel. They grab the Fae woman by her arms and carry her down the hall, disappearing past the corner. Sly turns back to the guests. "Sorry about that, everyone. How about a free round of drinks at the bar, huh?"

They cheer in response as they shuffle down the hallway for free alcohol. I'm glad no one's flashing Elias anymore, or trying to kill me, at least for now.

Sly turns to us both, eyeing my silver dress. "Taking your time getting this one to the dungeons, I see."

"On my way there right now," I say plainly.

"Good. We don't want another incident like that." He motions to the mess on the carpet, which is already being cleaned by staff, then adjusts his black tie. "I must open the doors. Get the prince to the warden and get back here before Thalius arrives."

"Wait. Thalius will be here?"

Sly smiles deviously. "Of course."

My jaw drops. I put it back in place.

Elias frowns but says nothing. Who cares? My mind is still on Thalius, the greatest keeper ever and…

Now I know what you're thinking. Iris, this isn't like you, losing it over a man. And you're right. It's not. But trust me, little bird, when you meet Thalius, you will understand!

Sly offers his arm to Callie. "Now dear, would you do me the honor of joining me to greet the guests?"

"Of course." The succubus blows me a kiss as she accompanies Uncle Sly toward the golden doors.

I yank Elias by his shackles. "Follow me."

He does, quieter than he's been all night.

We pass a few guests, all fans of Elias apparently, yadda yadda yadda, ah, and we're here, the dungeons.

I do my best impression of a game show model, holding my arms outstretched toward the dark, damp cells. "Welcome to your new home, vampire."

"Shade, technically."

"Whatever."

He sighs. "I'm half Fae, half vampire. That means I'm a Shade."

"Right, think I read about that…" I say, not trying to hide my sarcasm at all. Who does he think I am? A paranormal newbie?

He shakes his head. "You don't get it. My people used to be discriminated against, torn between two worlds, belonging nowhere. What were we but Shades of ourselves?" He pauses. "Even now, though laws protect us, few deem to follow them."

I yank his shackles again, leading him down a set of stone stairs, deeper into the dungeon. Blazing torches lining the stained walls light our way. "Boo hoo, your dark past made you a criminal, right? Don't think I haven't heard that story."

He stops, standing straight, eyes fierce. "I alone am responsible for my actions. I control my fate."

Huh. Haven't heard that one before. Not exactly anyway.

We continue our walk in silence, torches casting sinister shadows on the walls. Cries and whimpers ring out from the barred cells. Withered arms occasionally reach out and try to grab at my dress, but

I know the proper distance to keep. We pass by Fae, vampire, demon, crone and more. Even the young woman arrested moments ago upstairs. Race doesn't matter, only the crime, and as we make our way further underground, the bars become replaced by solid doors made of trimantium. Here, the most dangerous of criminals are kept, most locked away forever.

I take a quick detour to a more secret part of the dungeon, and something catches Elias's eye. A glowing light to the side, like moonbeams piercing the darkness.

"It can't be…" he whispers, leaving my side, following his gaze to a pedestal standing between two cells. A beam of bright light shines there, and within floats a silver sword.

"The Moonlight Sword," he says softly. "It was here all along. You never told me…"

I grin. "It was fun watching you try."

"But how? How is it here?"

I cross my arms, standing beside him. "Your father never lost the sword, Elias. He gave it to Sly for safekeeping, because he believed a weapon as powerful as the Moonlight Sword should be in no one's hands, not even a king's."

"Secrets upon secrets," murmurs Elias. "My family seems to never run out." He can't take his eyes away from the sword. He raises his hand towards the light. His fingers touch the beam.

He pulls away, hissing, his hand red and blistered.

"The beam will burn anything," I say. "Even Trimantium. Only the Moonlight Sword is, as you said, indestructible."

Elias flexes his hand, which is already healing. "You could have warned me."

I shrug. "You could have turned yourself in."

"Fair enough." He glances longingly at the sword one last time, before we continue walking deeper into the dungeon, his pale, shirtless body glistening in the torchlight. "Why keep the sword surrounded by criminals, though? Cocky much?"

"Sly says it's the safest place in the hotel," I explain. "Even if a criminal were to get their hands on it, which they wouldn't, they would never make it out of the dungeon. Not with the Warden, Fixers, and Sly himself keeping watch. Plus the magical reinforcement."

Elias nods. "That Sly does seem tricky. What is he anyway, a level ten demon?"

"No one knows," I say.

"Seriously?"

"Seriously. He's more ancient than anyone, and he never talks about his past. Trust me, I would know. Doing a school report on my family was a nightmare."

Elias chuckles. "Got it. No one messes with Sly. Must be why this place is so safe."

No one messes with Sly…

Wait a second.

Are you thinking what I'm thinking?

Could the White Rider wannabe have sensed *Sly* approaching? Is that why he left? But that would require some kind of premonition, fortune-telling crap, since my uncle appeared from thin air, and no one has those skills. Well, almost no one.

You and I are probably overthinking things.

Let's get back to the conversation. "Anyway, this section is only for criminals already sentenced to eternity. Those who will never leave. Here the sword is kept secret from the world, just as your father wanted."

Elias scans the dark walls, the damp stairs, the solid doors. "So no one's ever escaped before?"

"Never," I say proudly.

"Good. I like a challenge."

Of course he'd say that.

We stop at a dead end. As deep as deep can go. The bottom of the dungeon. Elias's cell. Nothing but the best for the number one most wanted criminal in the nine worlds.

He looks at the door before us and at the small room within. "Is that it?" he asks. "That's supposed to trap me?"

"That…" I nod. "And him."

A massive form emerges from the cell, a beast twice my height, black horns sprouting from his bald head, muscles bulging from under withered robes that kinda look like human skin. I've never asked. I don't recommend you ask either. Undone shackles hang on his wrists, and chains dangle from his belt, clattering against the stone floors. The Warden smiles. His teeth are sharp as daggers.

"Yeah, that might do it," says Elias quickly, his face a whole new level of pale.

I smile, gently pushing him forward and into his new quarters.

"You finally caught him," says the Warden, voice low and primal. "I always knew you would, Iris."

I pat him on the arm. "Thanks Big W."

"No. Thank you, Iris," says the demon, eyeing Elias like a piece of prime rib. "I have waited years for this day. Oh how long have I spent devising the methods of torture to use upon this one."

"Cool, but no torture yet, remember? He has to go before the council first."

The Warden gestures dismissively. "Minor details. Soon I will test the spleen stretcher."

"Sounds painful."

He beams. "Thank you."

Elias and I step into the cell, facing each other. I pull out the key for his shackles. For a moment, I am still, just standing there, taking it all in. "I guess… this is the end," I say.

He places his hand under my chin. "We had a good run, Iris. No regrets."

I nod, and slowly undo his shackles.

He massages his wrists, smiling.

For some reason, I smile back, but there's a bittersweet edge to it as I turn and leave, closing the door behind me. The Warden shuts it with a giant key. And then…

It is done.

My greatest challenge is over.

Elias Vane Spero has been caught.

Now a new enemy awaits.

But for a moment I feel… hollow. Empty. I wasn't expecting this.

I start to make my way back up, content to explore my complicated emotions at a later time, but Elias's voice stops me.

"Don't..." He steps forward, putting his face against the open grate in his door, barely big enough for his head. "Don't go after the White Rider."

"If he is a danger, I must."

"No." His eyes are dark and piercing and cold. "There are things you don't understand about the Council of Hunters."

I rush back down, placing myself against the door, my eyes inches from his, our breath melding together. We are so close, our bodies only separated by a sheet of metal.

"Then tell me," I whisper. "Tell me what I don't understand."

"Lix Tetrax," he murmurs, before raising his voice a fraction. "Not everyone on the council will wish for you to succeed," he says. "Some of them will wish you dead."

The heat of the torch licks my skin. "Who?"

He says nothing.

I slam my fist against the door. "Who!"

He does not speak for a while, and when he does his voice is barely audible. "I do hope we see each other again, Iris." He steps back, disappearing into the shadows, as if the cell has already swallowed him up.

I slam the grate closed. "You were always a liar." And talking to him was always a waste of time. I turn and run upstairs. But no matter how fast I run, his words follow.

The party, it seems, is about to start. I find Sly near the golden door, chatting with a pair of ladies, laughing and sipping on a purple drink.

"Lix Tetrax?"

He raises an eyebrow. "What?"

"Lix Tetrax?" I ask, breathless. "What is it?"

Sly clears his throat, eyes shifting in concern, as if he's looking for someone. Then his smile returns and he clutches my shoulder. "Never heard of it, darling. Why?"

Oh Uncle...

Why are you lying?

THALIUS

*M*y uncle, devious traitor that he is, escorts me into the ballroom, and for a moment all my worries fall away. The hall is magnificent, with murals of perfect athletes dancing on the ceiling, and white swans that swim in a pond black as night. The decorations are perfect, the staff more so. Employees of the hotel, all dressed in black, of course, seem to float through the space. Some carry delicious smelling *hors d'oeuvres* and purple drinks lit with a white fire that dances atop the crystal goblets. Others perfor feats of acrobatics, swinging from ropes up above, flipping through the air, while those down below breathe fire and dance in devilish masks. It's a feast for the senses. A spectacle to never forget.

I have been to such gatherings before when I was a child. Though lately, I've been too busy with hunting, and I wonder if my memory is simply hazy or if things are more impressive than ever. Uncle Sly does like to keep things interesting.

He waves a hand over his face and his features change. Black hair turns red in an instant. Pale skin turns freckled. Just simple illusion magic. Nothing I can't see through.

"Hiding from someone?" I ask suspiciously.

He grins. "Just going incognito. Easier to have fun that way." He waves a hand at me. "Want a touch up, love?"

"No," I say plainly. I enjoyed wearing magic like makeup as a teen, but lately I prefer truth to lies. Hunting criminals will do that, I suppose. If only my uncle felt the same...

I scan the crowd and notice he's not the only one to use a bit of illusion. It's quite common for those with the gift to cover up blemishes or scars, or to hire others to do it for them. Changing your appearance entirely, however, is highly illegal in all but the most necessary cases. But this is Sly, of course, and in the Black Lotus, Sly does what he wants.

His guests, hundreds of them, are dressed in the latest fashions of their kind, marveling at the splendor, often clapping and laughing. Some have outrageous hairstyles that defy gravity and nature, others have no hair at all. Some are covered in jewelry, others wear nearly nothing. But they all hide behind masks, thriving in ambiguity, whispering of the day's gossip.

I notice Callie, wearing a black mask herself, chatting with a dozen men and women. She is so at ease here, a master of the social graces. Personally, I'm more comfortable with my daggers.

"Ah," says Sly. "He is here."

I follow his gaze to the top of two arching stairways that meet together. And then...

I see him.

Thalius Gray.

The greatest keeper of all time. The leading member of the Council of Hunters. His long silver-blue hair falls perfectly over his shoulders. His pointed ears delicately frame his face. The white fur cloak he wears covers his back, but leaves his chest exposed, revealing cords of tanned muscle shining in the light. When he walks, it is both a dance and a challenge. When he speaks, it is a song on the wind more splendid than any bird's. A silver mask covers his face, but his eyes are ever watchful. The deepest green—like an emerald plucked straight from the deepest parts of the earth.

Oh Thalius...

I'm not drooling, am I? Please tell me I'm not drooling. I swear, I totally didn't have posters of this guy all over my teenage bedroom. Never.

He looks my way.

Our eyes meet.

My skin burns. My fingertips tingle.

When he walks down the stairs, the entire crowd parts before him, staring, whispering. And then I realize, they are all staring at me. Because that is where Thalius is headed. He holds out his arm. "May I have this dance, Iris?"

He knows my name! He… I mean… "Yes. Of course."

Thalius gestures to the orchestra in the corner, and they begin a slow melodic song. Gently, he takes my hand in his, and we begin to dance.

He tries to lead, but I don't let him.

It becomes a push and pull. Two opposites in perfect harmony.

Rumors say Thalius uses illusion to enhance his godly physique, but I'm calling bullshit. The man is fit.

"Impressive," says the keeper. "Not many can keep up."

I shrug. "Personally, this is a little slow for my taste."

"Oh." He raises an eyebrow and gestures to the orchestra once more. They increase the tempo, improvising, and we twirl through the room, drawing gasps and cheers. It is fortunate, I suppose, that Sly taught me to dance before he ever taught me to fight. 'Both are foot-work,' he would always say. 'One leads to the other.'

I pull away from Thalius, spinning on my own with the rising music, the world turning into a blur. I am lost within myself. The place I'm most free. And as the song ends, so do I stop, perfectly poised in an elegant pose, and the guests explode in applause.

Thalius claps loudest of all, drawing near once more. "Your skill at dance outdoes even your beauty, Iris."

"My skills at hunting are even greater," I say, panting, out of breath, totally trying to cover it up.

He rubs his chin thoughtfully, and I notice his nails are the same light blue as his hair. "Ah yes, it appears you have finally captured the Prince of Darkness."

"He is in a cell awaiting trial as we speak," I continue, glad my segue is working.

"Then I shall meet him soon," says Thalius, his voice as warm as honey. He has the greatest elegance of his people, the Fae. The most ancient of their bloodlines flows through his veins.

I put all that aside and focus on the task at hand. My palms are sweaty, but I'm sure it's simply from dancing. "I will be applying for watcher this year. Perhaps—"

"Watcher?" He blinks.

"Yes and—"

"But you're First Hunter. We need you out in the field."

"And I will be when needed. But—"

He takes me by the arms, pulling me to a private corner. I firmly yank myself free of his grasp in irritation. "I know I'm young for the position, but I'm better than half the council members already." My comment draws a few stares, but I don't care. I'm right.

Thalius chuckles. "Oh, Iris. It is not simply a matter of skill—"

"Why not?"

He lowers his voice. "I have heard of your ambitions, girl. You seek a seat on the council."

"Eventually—"

"There are only seven seats," he interrupts. "One for each major race."

"And I will represent the humans," I say fiercely.

He sighs, and in his eyes, I see something like disappointment. "But you are not human, Iris, are you? Half of you is mortal. The other half… something else. There is no room for one such as you on the council."

"But I…" the words don't come quickly enough. My throat tightens. "But… what of Aya'zee? She's on the council. She's half vampire, half Fae. A Shade."

"She is more vampire than Fae, believe me. Her bloodline is that of two major races. Yours, I'm afraid, is not. You are, to put it plainly, a mutt, and mutts have no place on the council." Thalius pats me on the shoulder, his voice smooth, condescending. "You are a hunter, Iris. It is what you do best. Why not stick with what you know?"

I bite my lip so hard it almost bleeds. "No."

"Excuse me?"

"I said, no." I step forward, meeting his gaze head-on. "I am the best hunter there ever was. Better, even, than you."

He laughs, but I can tell the stares we are drawing unnerve him. And then I understand. I challenge him. My very being challenges him. And he does not like being challenged.

"Delusional, are we?" he says for all to hear. Then he leans down, his words an angry hiss. "You will never be a watcher, girl. You will never sit on the council. Do you understand? You—"

A man in black grabs his arm, stepping between us. "Excuse me," says the stranger, his voice calm but strong. "But you seem to have forgotten your manners, sir."

Thalius scowls. "Sometimes a leader cannot be courteous," he says. "Sometimes they must be direct." He turns away then, scouring the crowd. "I've grown bored here anyway. Perhaps someone else will entertain me." He walks away, grabbing a goblet of wine from a passing server and downing the drink in a hurry. It isn't long before most people stop casting looks my way, returning to the festivities.

The dark stranger, however, remains at my side. He wears all black, from his fine pants to his thick cloak and his embroidered vest and gloves. A shadow lost on the marble. He smiles nonchalantly and holds out his hand. "May I have this dance, my lady?"

I study the little bit of his face not covered by his mask. The outline of his nose. The tanned skin of his cheeks. I don't recognize this man. He is most certainly not on the council. But is he a hunter? A watcher?

The stranger notices my pause. "I realize I'm no Thalius, but—"

I take his hand. "Thalius is overrated."

The stranger grins and puts a hand over the small of my back as we begin a slow dance. "Agreed. He was a complete turd to me growing up."

"Wait a second." I miss a step. "You grew up with Thalius Gray?"

"Of course. We're cousins, sort of, anyway, it's a long story."

I try to recall Thalius' family tree, but the branches are too many to count. "So what brings you here?" I ask.

He twirls me around. "Business, I suppose." He leans in conspiratorially, whispering in my ear. "To be honest, I am on a quest."

I notice how close we are. Bodies almost touching. "What kind of quest?"

"I am seeking something. A series of objects." His voice is light, playful. This is clearly a game to him, but at least games are fun.

"And what are these objects?" I ask, playing along.

His smile grows wider. "A cloak made of shadows, a bow carved from wind, and a sword bathed in light."

I try to keep a serious face. Emphasis on try. "And let me guess… one of these artifacts happens to be here."

He nods. "I believe so." He leans in closer, his breath hot against my ear. "Perhaps you can help me fetch it?"

I chuckle. "Sounds nice, actually. But I can't leave the party."

"Ah, trying to impress the council."

"Yes." I sigh, pulling away slightly. "Though clearly Thalius is not on my side."

He shrugs. "There are six other members, are there not? Certainly, they can't all be as blind to skill as my cousin." He pauses. "You captured Elias Vane Spero, didn't you? If you ask me, you should be running the entire organization."

I snicker, glancing to the side, scouring the crowd for other members of the council, but seeing none but Thalius. The sight that was once so lovely now makes my blood boil. "Unfortunately, it seems skill hardly matters."

The stranger nods thoughtfully. "Ah yes, as is often the case. Blood and birth are held above the rest." He pauses. "I myself am a second child. Second in line, as it were. Thus, I am not the heir to my family, and thus many opportunities are lost to me."

His story is entirely too relatable, and the truth feels like a stone in my stomach. "It should be different."

He grins, but the joy from his smile is gone. "Perhaps one day it will be."

There is something familiar about him. When the light catches his face, I could swear I know him. But I don't ask his name. Such things are not proper at a masquerade ball. One must choose to introduce themselves.

There is a moment of quiet before we speak again, while we simply dance to the slow, haunting music of the strings. "Perhaps this is too forward…" begins the stranger, "But I overheard you and Thalius speak. He said you were only half human."

My throat constricts. My hands twitch. "I… yes."

"Well, whatever your other half is… it's not noticeable in any way."

"Just a lesser monster," I say quickly. "Nothing important."

He eyes me carefully. "I see. I myself am of two worlds. I understand what it is not to belong." His voice is sad and tender.

I do not speak, for fear of breaking the moment between us.

The music slows. A violin plays the final note of the song.

And the stranger leans close once more. "I wish I could stay longer, but I'm afraid it's time for me to go." His lips brush my ear. "Oh, and thank you for showing me my father's sword." He pulls away, disappearing into the crowd, lost among the shadows.

What he said…

It can't be…

Elias?

MOONLIGHT

I know what you're thinking... Same thing I'm thinking. There's no way that was Elias. No one escapes the dungeons. No one. And if they did, it would take longer than one chapter, right?

Right.

So nothing to worry about except...

Shit.

Elias's father is Fenris Vane, half-brother to Kayla Windhelm, who is the mother of Thalius, which means...

Elias and Thalius are cousins.

Shit. Shit. Shit. Fu—

You may want to turn the page. Expletives continue for a while.

* * *

WHAT? Still here? Well, too bad for you, I burned the page you were looking for. I do have a reputation to uphold after all. Now, back to...

That bastard, Elias. Asshole was rubbing it in the whole time!

Now I know what you're thinking... Iris, how come a badass like you didn't see through his illusion spell? Why? Maybe because he was supposed to be in a dungeon that no one has ever escaped from. Like never ever.

Glad we got that cleared up, because I have a job to do.

He's still my mark. True, the dungeons are not my jurisdiction, but what do you think will happen to my reputation if people find out Elias escaped? It's like she never caught him, they'll say. She didn't even get to collect the bounty. They didn't even have a trial yet. I will not let that scheming vampire Fae tarnish my record.

I charge through the crowd, looking for the man in black, aka Elias. Of course, he's nowhere to be found in the ballroom. But where would he go?

The Moonlight Sword.

He must be looking for a way to steal the blade.

This is tricky. I need to catch him, but I also need to keep everyone at the hotel safe. Avoiding a mass panic is a plus. So… I might need back up. Like a succubus with a penchant for keeping people calm. And look, there she is, flirting with a pair of Fae twins with matching ponytails. (And they're totally hot so I'm really sorry to do this but…) I pull her aside, my voice low and urgent.

"We have a code purple," I whisper. "Repeat. We have a code purple."

She frowns, raising a perfectly plucked eyebrow. "A flying hippo is on the loose and terrorizing the hotel?"

"No. The other code purple."

She blinks. Her jaw drops. "Oh… but how? How could he—"

"No clue, but we need to find him." I snap my fingers, talking to the air. "Sly? Sly?"

He doesn't appear. Odd. He rarely fails to show up when I call him at the hotel. I scan the room, seeing if he's too busy smooching with someone or passed out drunk, but I catch no sight of him. Of course, he could have snuck off.

"Fine," I say, sighing. "We'll do this without him."

"Where do we start?" asks Callie, pulling her long red hair into a ponytail.

"I'll check the dungeons," I say. "You stay here, in case Elias shows up again. Explain the situation to all the Fixers, discreetly if you can."

She nods. "Should I tell Thalius?"

I glance at the smug watcher. His perfect face still makes my blood boil. His words still sting like a snakebite from hell. He's wrong about me, and I hate him, but...

"Yes. Tell him." I take a deep breath. "The council needs to be prepared. Also, Elias may be using illusion."

"You saw through his spell," she says, nodding.

I shake my head. "No, actually, I didn't."

"But that means..."

"He's even more powerful than we thought," I finish. "Be careful."

She nods, and we perform our secret handshake before parting ways. She walks over to Bobby and Poppy. I rush out of the ballroom, heading for my quarters.

Why my quarters, you may ask?

Because I need my gear.

I always keep a backup stash at the Lotus. Takes about a minute to reach my room, pop open the red trunk hidden behind a perfectly rendered painting of Starry Night (Sly says it's an original, that Van Gogh painted two and Sly bought one before anyone knew or cared about the famous artist), and dress for battle. Black leather armor and dark cape? Check. Black combat boots? Check. Daggers? Check. Now I'm ready to kick some vampire ass.

I tuck my black key necklace under my vest and make my way to the dungeons. I don't take the normal route, though. Don't want people to see a hunter decked out to the max and worry, now do I? So instead I take the secret passages carved into the bones of the hotel and known only to Sly, me, and a select few of the top Fixers. I would tell you where they are, but then Uncle would turn your guts inside out while playing 'you are my sunshine' on repeat, so how about no.

What I *can* tell you is the passages go past all the rooms in the hotel, allowing easy access and all that. So I'm making my way towards the underground when I hear—

"You were a bit harsh to the girl." A female voice, smooth and strong.

"I had to quell her ambitions." That voice…

Thalius.

I should keep going, but I can perhaps sneak a quick listen, can't I? Just for a sec? Oh look, a window into the room, right here on my path. Well, it's not really a window, per se. On the guest's side, it looks like a painting. On my side, it's the perfect way to spy on unsuspecting suspects.

Thalius sits in the shadows, sipping from a goblet. His companion, the woman, stands in front of him, pacing. I can't make out her features. She is a silhouette against the light of the balcony.

"With her bloodline," continues Thalius, "she can never be allowed into a position of leadership. Letting her walk free is already a gamble."

Lovely. They're talking about me. Spewing more hate on my lower blood. Well, I should really be—

"She seems quite in control to me," says the woman. Ooh, she sounds like she's on my side. Yay.

Thalius sighs, speaking softly. "The more she is allowed to rise in the ranks, the more she will learn, and she can never…" he pauses, his voice growing somber. "She can never discover her true heritage."

Wait. What?

"Hush now, Thalius," says the woman. "There are prying ears everywhere. Even within these walls."

She turns my way. Does she know about the passages? If she does, then she might find the hidden doors and…

I run. Whatever they were discussing, I wasn't supposed to hear, and I can't afford to be detained right now. So peace out, Thalius and mysterious woman. See ya later. I have an Elias to catch.

Which reminds me…

Now that I'm away from the guests, I put two fingers in my mouth and whistle. Theo may not be close, but he will heed my call. He will come.

Now, dungeon time. I jump out of a secret door in a secret location and make my way to the even more secret home of the Moonlight Sword. The halls are quiet here. The walls cold and damp. There is only me and the sound of my boots in the darkness, and I feel the shadows playing with my eyes.

Elias could be behind any corner.

He could be watching me, even now.

What if he has access to the passages somehow? What if he's setting a trap?

What if?

What if?

What if?

I see the pillar of light first. It's empty. The sword is gone.

A figure lies nearby in the darkness, writhing on the stone floor.

Elias?

No. I sprint forward. "Uncle!"

Sly trembles on the ground, eyes rolling into his head, foam spurting from his mouth as his body spasms repeatedly. A silver goblet lies tipped on its side by his hand, purple drink staining the floor. Poison! It must be. But what kind would affect him? I… I can't think about that now. Focus, Iris. Focus.

I fall to my knees by his side and cradle his head gently, trying to keep it still while I pull a blue vial from my cloak. "Easy now, Uncle. Everything will be okay, alright? Everything will be fine." Tears burn my eyes as I speak, and I pour the blue liquid down his throat, administering an antidote that should combat most poisons. I wait. Watch. But his symptoms don't change. The tears come in full force now.

There's still a chance the potion will work, but it will take a while for him to heal, and I don't have a while. I need to find Elias now! I need to warn Callie.

I'd use a cellphone if I could, but most technology doesn't work within the Black Lotus. Keeps people from snapping pics of the guests or intruders from capturing proof of the paranormal. Also made my teenage years less than awesome, in case you were wondering. So I'll need to run again. "I'll be back, Uncle," I whisper, kissing his forehead. "I'll be back, okay?"

A chill creeps into my skin, seeping into my bones. It's just the worry, right? The worry for my uncle. But then I see the frost spreading toward me. I see the flames flicker silver. And then...

I hear it.

> *He'll come in the night*
> *In armor of white*
> *Riding a steed of snow*

CHILDREN SINGING ON THE WIND. Their voices sound far away, as if they're coming from the main level of the Black Lotus. The White Rider is coming. Is this his doing? Did he have my uncle poisoned? I grit my teeth and follow the tune, drawing my daggers.

> *Three signs there are*
> *That mean he's not far*
> *Silver army in tow*

THE SONG GROWS LOUDER. It leads to the hall. To the ballroom. Where I left Callie. No. No. No!

> *First comes the frost*
> *Second the flame*
> *Third are the voices*
> *of those he has slain*

I BARGE INTO THE PARTY, looking for my foe. The guests have frozen, their bodies turned to ice, locked in whatever pose they had taken moments before. Many have their faces tilted upwards, listening to the haunting melody, looking for its source. Others point at the silver chandeliers and candles. It is so easy to mistake them for sculptures. To marvel at their beauty. Their realism.

But they are people.

Friends.

Family.

I run past them, searching for Callie and the rider. It is much darker now, the silver flames giving off barely any light, and I make my way through what feels like endless shadow, ice cracking beneath my heels. I recognize many of the masks I pass, but there are many others missing. Thalius is not here. Nor anyone else from the council. Perhaps the ice only freezes those of lower power. In which case...

"Iris!" Callie cries out, standing behind a pair of sculptures, Bobby and Poppy, both frozen with their hands inside their suits, reaching for weapons. The succubus runs to my side, a whip coiled around her arm. Thorns run down the length of her favorite weapon, clinging onto her flesh. They don't harm Callie, her enemies, however, don't fare quite so well. There was this one time, with an ogre, and that whip... well, it was quite a sight. But alas, a story for another time. Priorities.

"They all froze," says Callie frantically. "I couldn't stop it. It was like... it was like in the stories. The frost. The flame. The song."

"I know," I say calmly, trying to soothe her with my tone. "The White Rider is here."

Thud.

Thud.

Thud.

A horse rides out from the shadows above, where two stairways meet, carrying a rider of white. The steed rears onto its back legs, neighing, as its master lifts his silver sword. His eyes meet mine. And they are full of death.

When the rider speaks, his voice is low and dark, a whisper echoing his every word. "Elias is here, Iris. Hand him over to me, and I will undo what I have done." He points his sword at the people turned to ice, then at me. "What do you say, First Hunter?"

"Nope."

"Nope?"

"It's just, I've developed some trust issues lately," I say, twirling my daggers with a flourish. "Like with my uncle, and my teenage crush, so... how about you unfreeze them first, then I hand him over?"

"What?" he growls back.

I shrug. "I mean, I would just be more comfortable if you handled your part of the deal first. Or maybe like... maybe we could do it at the same time. Like you unfreeze them and I toss Elias your way, or... I don't know, how do you want to do this?"

He chuckles, the ground rumbling with his voice. "Few people make me laugh, Iris." He pauses. "Perhaps I'll kill you quickly as a kindness."

"We might have to work on your definition of kindness," I say.

He jumps off his steed, his body airborne as he prepares for his attack.

I push Callie to the side and dash the other way, barely avoiding his blow as he lands. His sword plunges into the ice rather than my heart, which is always a good thing. Callie and I slip apart, finding balance on opposite sides of the ballroom. I raise my daggers, turning to face the rider. I move my eyebrows in a pattern, signaling Callie to run.

She signals back. *No.*

I signal: *You're no fighter. Run.*

She signals. *No. We're friends.*

I raise both eyebrows twice. Then my right once. Then—

The White Rider stares at my dancing eyebrows, frowning. "I must admit," he says, "in all my years, I have never seen this before. Clearly, you two are close." His cheeks creep up in a smile. "If you will not surrender Elias for them. Perhaps you will for her."

He turns on my friend, walking her way, his sword scraping the ice, sending a screech through the air. Total horror movie move, but it works.

I run after him. On a slippery floor, because, duh, ice. I'm not fast enough. "Run!" I yell.

Callie stays her ground, uncoiling her whip. Her eyes are red and fierce. "You froze my friends," she spits at him, her eyes shifting to Bobby and Poppy and the others she befriended that I never did. Her voice is low, full of rage and passion. "You will bring them back."

The rider smiles.

And she strikes at him with the thorn-whip.

He avoids her attacks with ease, leaning away from her blows.

I must do something to slow him down. Anything. "Run," I yell again, but she doesn't listen.

"Run," I yell, but she keeps fighting.

I toss my dagger at his head. Without even looking, he moves out of the way, and my blade bounces against his horns, flying past him on a new trajectory.

Hitting Callie in the shoulder.

She falls to her knees, clutching at my weapon, blood running down her dress.

"No!" I roar. "Face me, rider. Face me, coward."

He does not stop. He does not turn.

I leap into the air, remaining dagger aimed at his ribs.

He slides forward, faster than I have ever seen, as if he can glide on the ice, skating on it with ease. He is upon Callie in an instant, silver blade in hand.

She looks at me one last time.

"I'm sorry," she whispers.

And he runs the blade through her chest.

DARKNESS

*T*his has happened before.

A friend.

A monster.

A violent death.

Unwanted memories scratch below the surface of my mind. They are like wraiths trying to break free from a frozen lake. I drown them out. Bury them deep in the depths of my consciousness.

I understand you want to know more, little bird.

And perhaps one day I'll tell you.

But for now, know this…

Some truths take time.

And right now, I have little.

SOMETHING IN ME SNAPS. A lock. A door. Energy I have never felt flows through my body, clearing my mind, filling my tendons with power and speed. Everything within me burns with fire. Everything outside me feels too slow. Primal instincts take the lead. Years of training and practice possess my mind and body.

I drop to my knees, sliding forward with incredible momentum, propelling myself with impossible force. The shadows seem to follow in my wake, gathering behind me in a trail of darkness, driving me onward. I slice out with my dagger, and the blade extends into steel dark as night.

The rider leaps away.

I jump, launching ten feet into the air after him, a cloak of endless shadow behind me. My dark sword meets the silver blade, and for the first time, I see something new in the rider's eyes.

Panic.

"What are you?" he whispers.

His words glance off me. I am not one for talking or planning or persuading. That is better left to people and right now I am no person. I am a force of nature itself.

The rider knows. I can see it in his eyes. He fights not with ease, but with caution, and for a moment we are equal as we dance in the air, black and white clashing in a room of frost.

A pained groan comes from below. It pulls me away from the force that entraps my mind. The succubus rolls on the floor. Callie! She yet lives.

I fall to her side, studying her wounds in an instant. My dagger took her in the shoulder. The silver blade took her in the chest but missed her heart. She is full monster, unlike me. She may actually survive this.

But she needs a healer.

"I'll get you out," I whisper in her ear.

She nods, her eyes and mouth closed in pain, tears streaming down her perfect face.

The more I think of my friend, the more my power fades, the more I am myself again. My blade turns into a dagger once more.

The White Rider lands behind us, his steps light on the ice. "I see now," he says, voice echoing through the hall, "why you rose so quickly through the ranks. I wonder, who else knows your true nature."

I don't understand what he's saying. I don't understand what just happened.

Only one thing matters.

Callie.

I lift her in my arms and fling her over my shoulder, leaving my right hand free as I run toward the door.

The rider growls. "We are not done yet, hunter."

An unnatural wind storms through the room. Snow falls from the dark ceiling.

And then the ice itself moves. It grows. Humanoid figures rise from the frost, like skeletons of glass. The first to manifest charges my way, striking with claws.

I spin past the creature, stabbing my dagger in its back, and it shatters, exploding into shards of ice. More of the beasts come my way. Dozens of them.

I take them out one at a time, but they are never-ending. A horde of mindless creatures. A silver army.

How is the rider doing this? Is he really the monster from legends?

"Tell me where to find Elias," he commands. "Tell me, and I will stop my assault."

I try to say something witty, but well, I'm busy fighting off twenty ice soldiers while holding a succubus over my shoulder. If only there were two of me.

Which reminds me. Perhaps it's time I send another signal. I shatter an ice creature with a kick to the face, then whistle toward the door. A meow comes in response.

Yes.

He's here.

The doors fling open wider. And then emerges—

"Is that a kitten?" asks the rider, eyebrow raised.

A shaggy white kitten with spots of black and brown runs into the hall, his little paws carrying him to my side, his blue eyes squinting in determination.

I turn to the rider, grinning. "That's no simple kitten. That's a manticore travel size, bitch."

The kitten shifts, growing to three times my size, white wings unfurling, blue mane swaying in the unnatural wind. He roars, shattering the ice creatures with his voice.

Theo has found me.

"Take Callie to safety," I say, holding her up.

He bites down gently on her clothes, carrying her like he would a baby kitten, but I catch a hesitation in his sapphire eyes.

"I'll be fine, boy," I say. "Go."

He growls and sprints out the room, ice cracking beneath his claws. I would catch a ride, but then the White Rider would follow. I need to keep him distracted.

So I clench my jaw and raise my dagger. "You like to pretend you're the big bad White Rider, but guess what?"

He smiles, stepping closer. "Enlighten me."

"The real White Rider has no fear," I say, rushing forward, locking my blade with his. "He wouldn't flee from old Uncle Sly. Yet you ran away like a purple baby hippo when you felt his presence at the crone's party."

"I did not—"

"With your little tail hanging between your legs." I hold up two fingers and move them like legs.

He roars, pushing me back, swinging his blade at my torso.

I flip backwards, avoiding his blow. "And this time," I continue. "You had Sly poisoned before your arrival." I strike low, cutting at his knees.

The rider slides away. "You assume too much, hunter. Perhaps it was dear Elias who poisoned your uncle. Or maybe one of your precious council." His cold eyes survey the frozen sculptures. "How appropriate that I see none of them here. I wonder, what schemes do they carry out elsewhere in the hotel while we fight?"

That's a good point, actually, but I can think about Thalius and the other keepers later. Right now, I have ass to kick and a friend to save.

I slide forward, spinning like a tornado of carnage, a volcano of death, a tsunami of—

The rider easily sidesteps my attack.

What?

He's toying with me, the bastard. This isn't good. Somehow, I matched him in power when I was all covered in shadow and stuff, but now he's always three steps ahead. Make that five steps. Make that...

Why hasn't he killed me yet?

Not that I'm complaining. Just wondering.

"You have potential, Iris," he says. "The council will never allow your true power. But I will. Let me teach you."

Ah, so that's why.

"No thanks," I say. "Trust issues, remember."

His eyes fall. "You think you have a place amongst them," he says, gesturing to the frozen guests. "But one day, you will understand. They will never accept you."

I purse my lips in mockery. "Aw, was someone mean to you? Did they hurt your feelings?" I dash around him, striking at his arms. "Is that why you're after Elias? Did the two of you go on a date and he left without saying goodbye?"

"You know nothing of me," he roars, sliding toward me in an instant, stabbing his sword through my cloak and pinning me to the ice. He aims a metal fist at my face, ready to crush. "Elias is—"

"Did someone call my name?" The teasing voice comes from above.

The rider looks up and smiles. "Finally," he hisses, blue eyes glinting, fixed on his prey.

Elias Vane Spero stands on top of the chandelier, dressed all in black, a silver blade in his hand.

The Moonlight Sword.

It glows in the darkness. It's movements echo on the wind.

"Now, love," says Elias, winking at me. "How about you go check on your friend while I settle matters here."

I roll to the side, tearing my cloak but breaking free as I stand. "I'm settling matters myself, thank you very much," I say, twirling my dagger.

The Prince of Darkness shrugs. Then he leaps down, his new sword aimed at the rider. The creature of legend grins, as he rends his weapon free and jumps up, their blades clashing in the air. Steel rings throughout the hall. A light pulses in the darkness.

The Moonlight Sword. It's glowing, resisting the attack. This is the real blade. The one wielded by Elias's father before him.

The rider and vampire pull apart, landing on opposite sides of the hall. Elias gestures at me. "Ever heard of a distraction, Iris?"

"Word sounds familiar."

"Use this one to run."

"Listen to him, hunter," says the White Rider.

Silly men. The First Hunter never backs down. Only one problem... Who is my target now? Both of them? Neither of them? Damn, Elias confuses me. Why did he return? If he stole the sword, why didn't he flee?

The prince lunges forward, striking at the rider, sword gleaming in the shadows. The blade makes him faster than before, stronger. He seems almost a match for the rider. Almost.

"My dear Elias," says the creature, "will you never learn?" He grabs the prince's head.

And slams it into a wall.

So hard the marble breaks.

Once.

Twice.

The prince falls, the side of his face torn open, his eyes twitching. The sword slides out of his hand. He tries to reach for the blade, but the rider kicks him across the forehead, causing him to go limp.

Elias may be a criminal, but he deserves a trial. Not this.

I run forward, but I am not close enough.

The rider chuckles, grabbing the Moonlight Sword and lifting his prey by the collar, dragging the prince behind him into the shadows. "We shall meet again, hunter."

He steps into the shadows. And—

No. Not this time buddy.

I leap forward, hitting the ice, letting my momentum carry me, and grab the whip Callie left behind off the floor. I lash toward the darkness. The whip finds purchase. And I pull myself forward after them. This time, when I reach the shadows, I do not hit a wall. This time, I fall.

And land in a world of night.

A world of cold and frost.

A blizzard rages around me. The sky is dark and full of stars. The floor is black ice, but not slippery like before. Gray trees sprout from the ground, showing no signs of leaves, no signs of life. They are withered dead things, their branches curling toward me like claws. They surround the area, stretching out into long forests. In their depths, I see red eyes flash and hear the growls of wild beasts. None approach. Instead, they flinch if they ever draw too close.

Behind me stands an obsidian door etched in markings. It leads to nowhere, standing isolated, tall enough for three of me. It must be a portal of sorts, the way I fell in here. In front of me, the whip curls around a root piercing the ice. My handhold, as it were. It's cracked, almost broken from my weight.

In the distance, the rider drags Elias over a path of snow, upwards toward a central hill. There, a mighty tree grows, larger than the rest, its roots visibly sprouting from the earth like gray worms. Its branches reaching so high I cannot see their end. A Mother Tree. I have seen the like before, but never one such as this. A Dead Tree.

This one gives no life. Instead it seems to suck it from the land, feeding off the earth like a parasite. It's thick trunk pulses, like a bulging womb. Dark crimson sap oozes from its bark, like festering boils. There's something within. Something inside.

Iris...

The voice is a whisper in my mind. A warm caress in the harsh cold.

Iris...

No. Focus. Focus.

The rider hasn't noticed me yet. Good. He's too cocky to consider I'd be able follow him. I can use that. Activate sneak mode. Be one with the shadow. Move like ninja.

You get the picture.

I crouch low, creeping quietly over the snow and ice, climbing a

67

short cliff that runs parallel to the rider's path. Soon, I am above him, watching as he pulls Elias to the base of the tree. "My dear friend," says the rider. "Finally, your blood will be put to proper use." He grabs the prince's arm and holds it up to the trunk. A handprint is carved into the bark, a spike in the center.

The rider pushes Elias's hand onto the mark, piercing it through, tearing it open. The vampire's blood flows out, spreading from the carving, flowing into thousands of crimson lines across the tree. He's feeding it, I realize. Feeding it blood.

What kind of messed up shit is this?

A part of me kinda wants to sit tight and see what happens next, but I won't because Elias is looking paler than usual, and well…

Blood + tree = bad.

That much is clear. So…

I can't beat the rider. But maybe I can stop this dark ritual. Only one idea pops into my head. One totally not foolish, brilliant idea.

STEALTH ATTACK!

I jump of the cliff, dagger in hand.

The rider notices me at the last moment, spinning out of the way, avoiding my sneaky maneuver, swinging the Moonlight Sword at my neck.

Don't worry, little bird. All part of the plan.

I curl into a ball, saving my neck, and land beside Elias, grabbing him into my arms. As the rider strikes again, I leap away, running madly toward the obsidian door. Whatever magicks he used to teleport here, I don't possess. But I do have a trick of my own.

I pull the necklace Sly gave me free from my vest and grip the black key. Behind me, the blizzard takes form, turning into a steed of snow beneath the rider's feet. He charges, gaining, his strikes cutting my cloak to ribbons.

I dash forward, shoving my key into the obsidian lock as I fall, and I tumble into the Black Lotus, kicking the door closed behind me.

I crash into the marble wall of the ballroom, dropping Elias, panting, my chest heaving uncontrollably. The silver flame is gone. Bright torchlight has returned. All around me, the frozen guests begin to melt, slowly moving rigid limbs. The ice breaks away, revealing warm flesh, and people gasp for air, their eyes wild, disoriented. Poppy and Bobby return to form, whipping out daggers from their suits as if they never missed a beat, only to look around confused.

There are murmurs.

Then shouts.

Then screams.

So much for avoiding a mass panic.

Thalius bursts into the room, dozens of watchers in tow. His eyes nearly explode when he notices Elias unconscious at my side.

"Took you long enough," I say, grinning, not even caring about the inevitable hit to my rep.

He scowls, pointing my way. "They have stolen the Moonlight Sword," he spits. "Arrest them both."

Wait…

Arrest who now?

SLY

*N*ow, we both know I didn't steal the Moonlight Sword. Stealing is just not my thing. I mean, when I was ten I snuck a chocolate bar from Sly's personal stash, and as I was putting it in my mouth he snapped his fingers and the chocolate turned into gray worms so…. Yeah… traumatized. Definitely not a thief.

That honor goes to Elias.

I tell Thalius as much.

"Then where is the blade now?" he asks, surrounding the prince and me with twelve damn good watchers, aka elite hunters. Everyone else is evacuated from the ballroom as we speak, though it's more like they run out in terror. Sly and Callie are nowhere to be seen.

"The White Rider took it," I say, as a watcher confiscates my dagger and slips completely unnecessary handcuffs on my wrists, then shackles the unconscious Elias.

Thalius raises an eyebrow. "The White Rider? The fairytale?"

"He was here," I continue. "Or at least, someone pretending to be him. He froze all the guests and—"

"All except you."

I shrug, raising my cuffed hands innocently. "The power didn't affect anyone over level eight. Now, if you don't mind, I really need to check on my friend and uncle—"

Ten watchers point their weapons at me in unison, halting me in place. Huh. I guess they do mind.

"Just ask the guests!" I yell. "They must have seen something!"

A watcher whispers into the keeper's ear.

He smirks. "We did ask the guests," says Thalius. "One moment they remember dancing, the next they see you and Elias together. No rider. Just you."

"He was here."

Thalius starts to pace around me in a circle, gesturing to his comrades. "Let me make sure I'm understanding this correctly. A fairytale monster crashed the party and, using impossible magical abilities, stole the Moonlight Sword from Elias, who stole it earlier on his own. The First Hunter—that being you—tried your best to stop him, but failed, despite your reputation as one of the greatest fighters of this age. Does that sound about right?"

Well, when you put it that way…

"What do you think happened?" I ask plainly.

Thalius smiles devilishly. "I think you and the Prince of Darkness colluded. You brought Elias to the dungeons and left him with a means to escape. While he stole the sword, you incapacitated everyone at the ball, releasing a paralysis toxin into the air and poisoning your uncle. Then you and Elias reunited, but argued over the possession of the blade, thus his torn face. You won the battle and hid the sword before we arrived. That, Iris, is what I think happened."

Note to self: Never ask your new arch nemesis what they think happened. Ever.

The watchers nod along, clearly convinced by the keeper's argument, or they're sucking up. Either way, I'm screwed.

"So yeah," I begin, "That's completely wrong and—what's that?"

Thalius shoves a trimantium tazer into my gut and… well, I don't remember, because I was freaking tazed! That devious asshole. I can't believe I ever admired him. And the things I did while looking at his poster. Just… yuck.

Oh, you want to know what happens next, don't you? Right. So…

"GOOD MORNING, LOVE," says Elias, his shirt off for some reason, revealing his black tattoos. "I would have made breakfast but…" he raises two hands shackled to the wall behind him and shrugs.

My head feels like a gargoyle fell on it, and it takes a moment for white specks to leave my vision. "Where are we?" I ask, my tongue heavy and slightly numb.

"Don't you recognize it, Iris? It's—"

"No," I shake my head, taking in the dark walls, the trimantium door and shackles. "This can't be—"

"The Black Lotus dungeons," finishes Elias cheerfully. "Complete with pissing pot," he gestures to the right. "Shitting pot." He gestures to the left. "And… I don't know what that is actually. Some kind of chair perhaps?"

I sigh. "It's a chopping block. In case they want to execute you out of sight."

Elias nods thoughtfully. "Well, we have one of those too then." I realize his face is already healed, his skin pale in the little light we get through the open grate in the door.

I yank on my chains, but of course all I accomplish is bruised wrists. "Why are we in here?"

"Pretty sure Thalius—"

"No. Why are we in here together? Protocol dictates isolation for all criminals above level five."

"Guilt by association," says Elias, voice low. "For whatever reason, Thalius hates you. Likely, he believes the more people see you with me, the more they will assume you abetted my crimes."

Yeah… what's up with Thalius anyway? Is he really that pissed off I challenged him at the party? Or is it something else? Something about my true heritage?

Either way, his plan is stupid. No one will believe him because… "I would never help you," I say quickly.

Elias shrugs. "And yet, here I am. Alive because of you."

"You remember what happened?"

"Pieces here and there," he says softly. "Thank you... for what you did."

I stare at him a moment, thinking. "What does the rider want with you?"

"I have my theories—"

"Tell me."

He leans back, resting his head against the wall. "When he brought me to the tree I felt..."

"A presence," I say.

He nods. "Whatever it is, it wants my blood. To become stronger perhaps. Maybe to break free."

I remember the bulging Dead Tree, growing like a womb as it fed off his strength. "But why you?" I ask. "Why specifically you?"

"I am the High Prince of Hell," says Elias, his tone full of disdain. "Royal blood of both Fae and vampire runs through my veins, haven't you heard?" He slumps down, chuckling with no warmth. "I suspect our rider requires that particular cocktail for his needs. An Elias on the rocks, as it were."

"You have other family," I say, fidgeting, my hands itching to have my daggers back.

"Well, perhaps I'm the easiest to capture. Being on the run with no friends and all that."

I grimace. "You seemed to have quite the fan club upstairs."

"They'd enjoy watching me burn as much as seeing me walk free," he says somberly, his dark hair drifting over his eyes. "To them I am entertainment. Nothing more."

His words hover in the air, and then, trapped in the darkness of a cell, I see him in a new way. A prince who lost his birthright, who pushed everyone away, living in cage of his own making. Alone.

Well, alone except for me.

"Anyway, as much as I would like to join you in your brooding, I have things to do, people to find, so... goodbye," I say, pressing my feet against the wall for leverage, pushing and pulling at the same time with all my strength. I need to check up on Callie and Sly.

"Oh," whispers Elias, astonished. "I never tried that maneuver before."

"It's really... ugh... quite... argh... simple. You... ah... need to—" My legs buckle and I fall on my ass, the chains smacking me on the way down.

Elias chuckles, clapping awkwardly with cuffed wrists. "Would you care to demonstrate again, hunter? I fear I may have missed the part where your plan works."

"Shut it," I hiss, preparing to try again.

"You know," Elias begins softly, his voice smooth and sultry. "You and I are going to be in here a long time. With oh so little to do. Perhaps, with you being a woman, and me being... well, me, the two of us can—"

"Nope. Never. Not in a million years."

He grins smugly. "What about a million and one?"

"Nope. I don't date criminals."

"Oh, we can skip the dinner and flowers if you'd like," he says, gesturing to bucket number one and bucket number two.

I try to slump down in a comfortable position but... "Man, these cells suck. How do you, like—"

"Stay here for all eternity?" asks Elias. "Well, don't fret, dear Iris. I am quite the expert at being imprisoned."

I freeze. "That's right. You escaped here before. How?"

"Using a means no longer possible," he says. "One I would rather not divulge."

"Was it a mirror?" I ask plainly.

He glances around innocently. "A mirror?"

"Yeah, cause you're a vampire. Mirrors are like portals for you."

"True. It's the reason we don't show up in reflections. It's why—"

"Yeah," I cut him off. "I'm aware. First Hunter over here for a reason. So was it—"

"Yes. Fine. It was a mirror," he blurts out, breathing heavily.

I perform my WTF face. "Like... how? Where did you put it?"

He swallows uncomfortably. "In areas I would rather not discuss."

"Like was it a tiny one, like under your molar? Or was it... oh no..."

"Yes, fine. It was in my anus, you happy now, hunter? You happy that you know my secret escape plan," he yells.

I cringe like I'm about to eat worms instead of chocolate again. "But that... that must have been so painful."

"Well, it wasn't a spring picnic, I can tell you that."

I nod. "But doesn't the Warden check for that? Like, right away."

"Yes, but with the proper muscle contractions and illusion—"

"Got it, so... why didn't you... um... replace this mirror after you escaped?"

He sighs. "I misplaced it while reclaiming my father's sword. And in case you hadn't noticed, you don't exactly have mirrors small enough to fit my bum hole hanging around."

Right so...

I'm just going to pretend that conversation never happened. But hey, you wanted the whole story, right?

"Out of curiosity, how *did* you reclaim the Moonlight Sword?" I ask.

He grins smugly. "I realized the deadly beam of light must have had a switch, an on and off button, as it were. How else could someone have placed the sword within? Indeed, there was a mechanism at the back of the pedestal, hidden beneath the stone. I had to solve a puzzle to access the switch, but it wasn't particularly challenging for a person of my intellect and skill."

I roll my eyes.

A tap.

Like stone crumbling.

The wall between Elias and I begins to bulge out in the center.

I signal to Elias with my hands.

He mouths, *What?*

I mouth back.

He squints.

I sigh.

The wall begins to break open.

"What?" whispers Elias. "What are you trying to say?"

"I…"

Rock falls away. A head of black hair pops out. It turns until—

"Uncle Sly?"

He tumbles through the wall, landing in the dirt. "Hello, my dear," he says, spitting out a mouthful of mud, quickly dusting off his black tux. He wears shackles like ours. Actually, his are fancier, engraved with ancient runes.

"You're okay," I say, tears welling in my eyes.

"Okay?" asks Sly, shaking his manacled hands. "This is not bloody okay."

"I meant the poison…"

"Oh, yes. Thank you for the antidote, my dear," he says, kissing me on the cheek. "I heard you saved me when I was tossed into the cell next to yours, complete with magic draining attire of course." He raises his fancy shackles.

"What the hell is going on?" I ask, clasping his hands in mine.

"It's a bloody coup," he says, pacing dramatically. "Someone wants the Black Lotus for themselves. Someone orchestrated this entire incident. Poisoned me. Framed you."

"Thalius," I say in dramatic serious mode.

Sly rubs his chin. "Maybe. Or maybe he's a pawn, playing someone else's game without even realizing it. Either way, he was the only council member to stick around for the party. Odd, to say the least."

"So," says Elias, standing. "What were you saying, Iris?"

I blink. "What?"

"While he was digging through?"

"Oh. I was saying this is some Count of Monte Cristo shit."

"That's…" His jaw drops. "It could have been anything coming through that wall and that's what you had to tell me?"

I shrug, because, like, wasn't it obvious? So… "How are we getting out of here, Uncle?"

"Well…"

Elias walks forward, joining our little huddle. "Right. You built this place, didn't you? You must know a secret passage."

"No secret passages, sorry." He gives Elias a wink. "No mirrors either."

"Wait. You heard—"

"Oh, half the dungeon heard it, my prince," says Sly, breaking into a laugh.

Elias makes a sort of low growling noise, like brooding perfected. "Okay," he continues, pointing at the new hole in the wall. "How about you dig us out of here then?"

"Sadly, that was an already weak spot I've been meaning to fix," says Sly. "Digging around the door will be quite impossible."

"Have you seen Callie?" I ask.

Sly shakes his head. "She's with the healers. At least she was."

"And Theo?"

"Escaped. Thalius sent hunters after him."

My hand folds into a fist. I just really wish I had Thalius's face to go along with it. "That's it," I say firmly. "You're telling me everything, Uncle. The council. The White Rider. Lix Tetrax. Everything."

"Well…" he scratches uncomfortably at his throat. "It's really not that—"

I grab him by the collar, glaring into his eyes. "Tell me. Now. Or I will never forgive you."

"Not even if—"

"Yes, not even if you give me another llama."

He sighs, slipping out of my grasp. "Very well then. It all started with…"

He begins to talk and—

The ceiling explodes, crushing us and…

I'm just messing with you. Sorry. He tells me everything. But just so you know…

In the end, it may have been better if he told me nothing at all.

SHADOW'S BANE

*S*tory time, little bird.

Have a seat by the imaginary fireplace. Kick your feet up on the chopping block. If you need to use the restroom, remember bucket number one and bucket number two are located close by for your convenience. Now, relax and enjoy the tale of two brothers.

Bro number one is mean as a viper. True stone-cold gangster. Has a crew like no other, and by the way, he's an angel. *The* angel, actually. Some would call him a god if they called him anything.

Bro number two is… well, he's basically like bro number one, just a little less impressive. Folks call him Lucian Vane. Maybe you've heard of him. Maybe not.

Together they run the streets of the Silver City, aka angel land, aka heaven.

But one day, Lucian grows tired of living in his brother's shadow, so he makes a play for the kingdom.

Bro number one, who doesn't even have a name because he's so hardcore, doesn't like that very much. So he and his squad beat the shit out of Lucian and all his stupid supporters. They don't kill them though, because bro number one takes care of his family. That's his creed or something or… look, I don't remember. Point is…

Instead, he puts a curse on Lucian and his team. Makes it so the Earth's sun burns their skin. Makes it so they need human blood to survive. Then he does one better and exiles them from the Silver City. Tosses them and their broken dreams to some place called Inferna, aka hell. Best part is, there are no humans on Inferna. Only some poor souls called the Fae.

Worst part is, Lucian's squad is like, this is our turf now, you hear? So he and his sons lead a war against the Fae, massacring that shit. They take most of Inferna for themselves and make the Fae into their slaves. Totally not cool, but hey, history sucks sometimes, you know?

So listen up, because Lucian and his peeps still need human blood and stuff, so they use mirrors to hop on over to Earth and do some biting. Soon enough, they're not called angels anymore. Nope. I think you can guess what we call them now, can't you, little bird?

Vampires.

Fast-forward a few millenniums and Lucian conducts a long and slightly convoluted plan to return to the Silver City. Spoiler Alert: He fails.

Because... oh I should wrap this up, huh? Right. Short version: He fails because Arianna Spero and Fenris Vane, aka Elias's parents, kill him. Then the Fae and vampires reconcile their differences and live together happily ever after. Yay!

The end.

Or so I thought...

Because now Sly is telling me something else. He's telling me...

"They say Lucian and his sons were the first vampires," he whispers, eyes dark. "They are wrong."

"Don't tell her!" yells Elias, smashing into my uncle, knocking him into the wall.

"She needs to know," he spits back, slipping away from the prince.

Elias tries to follow, but I jump between them, using my body to separate them. The way they stare at one another, it suddenly clicks... "You've met before," I say softly. "You've discussed this. You've discussed me."

Sly clears his throat. "We may have spoken on an occasion."

"Briefly," adds Elias.

Their secrets are really starting to piss me off. "Why?" I ask.

"Lix Tetrax," says Elias. Right. Like that explains it...

Sly nods. "Elias needed help with a particular problem. In exchange, he gave me some advice. Don't tell Iris the truth."

I frown at the prince. "Thanks," I say sarcastically.

Elias meets my gaze, his voice low. "If you know, they will come for you."

"They?"

"The enemy."

"And they are..." hold on a second. I'm having a brain moment. Wait, you too? Awesome. You thinking what I'm thinking?

Cause I'm thinking...

"Lix Tetrax is the enemy," I say.

Slowly, Elias and Sly both nod.

"They're a cult of sorts," says uncle.

Elias shakes his head. "More of a Holy Order."

"An organization really."

"A secret group of individuals."

"More like a sect."

"Or a book club specializing in evil."

"Okay!" I yell. "I get it." Deep breaths, Iris. Deep breaths. "Now... why the secrecy?" I glare at Elias. "You're the one who told me to ask my boss about Lix Tetrax."

The prince nods. "I wanted you to know they exist. I wanted you to be prepared." He pauses. "I knew you would never trust me, but perhaps you would trust your uncle or someone on the council."

"Right," I say. "So, what's the problem?"

"The secret," says Elias. "If you discover their secret, they will come for you. They will find you. And they will give you two choices. Join them or die."

His eyes are vicious, filled with harsh sincerity.

"But if that's true, then how are you two..."

Sly sighs. "There's a reason I rarely leave the Black Lotus, darling."

"Because you're all powerful here," I say slowly. "At least without the shackles." I turn to Elias. "But you... you're no match for Sly. You couldn't evade them unless..."

Cold pricks my skin. "Unless you joined them."

He says nothing for a time, his features cold and distant. "I..." The words seem physically painful to speak. "I had two options. Die. Or join Lix Tetrax and try to destroy them from within. As you can see, I chose the latter."

My lips part. "Is that why you did all those things? Why you were on the most wanted list?"

"In part," he says. "Some of the things you've heard have been exaggerated, others twisted against me. All by those who would like to see a Prince of Hell beheaded."

I rub my forehead. "But how can Lix Tetrax know who to hunt down? I mean, do they have a new member GPS? Or are they more all-knowing, kinda like the IRS?"

"Neither," says Elias. "We are all bound by the secret. It is a part of us. A mark. We are like strands twined together, and those with the knowledge can follow the threads to their source."

Sure... suppose that makes a kind of sense. Maybe. Anyway... "I'm the First Hunter," I say, standing tall. "Let them try and come for me. Let them dare."

Elias shakes his head. "Iris, there is no need—"

"Lix Tetrax might scare you, Prince of Darkness," I say, pointing at his face. "But they do not scare me. So tell me. Tell me this secret!"

Sly runs a hand through his black hair. "Are you sure another llama won't—"

"No."

He sighs. "Very well. Lucian and his sons were not the first vampires. There was another before them. The first bearer of the curse."

He looks out through the grate, toward the dim light in the hall. "You see, Lucian and his brother were not always rulers of the Silver City. No, they too once had a father. And one day, they decided to overthrow their immortal ruler. They could not kill him. So instead they cursed him first. Burn him in the sun, they did. Starve him of blood, they did. And yet he would never die. Only weaken. And so finally they locked him away in a place now forgotten. The secret of his very existence itself they cursed, so anyone bearing its knowledge could be found and killed. He is the Forgotten One. The Unseen Lord. The First Vampire."

I sit down, my heart thundering in my chest. "So Lix Tetrax protects the secret. Keeps the Unseen Lord locked away."

Sly chuckles, though there is no joy in his voice. "If only... Some still follow the old code. But others walk a new path. You see, when Lucian and his brother quarreled, they lost sight of the task, and lost control of Lix Tetrax. Then the Order changed. Tore itself in two. Lix Tetrax and a new sect. Those who deserted joined with a cast of vampires who are not pleased to share Inferna with the Fae. Together, they call themselves the Unfettered. And they are seeking the Forgotten One. Seeking him with all their power."

He sits down in the dirt. "For it is said, if he is ever freed, an eternal darkness will cover the land. And vampires will have dominion over all the worlds."

Elias nods. "There's more. I'm not privy to the great mysteries of my Order, but of this I am certain: Lix Tetrax influences the Council of Hunters in secret. Our leader, called the Tempest, controls the keepers like a puppet master pulling at strings."

I sigh, rubbing my temples. "And this Tempest is..."

"Never met them," says Elias. "The Order communicates with messages whenever possible. Rarely in person."

Of course...

Like a magician Sly conjured a bottle of rum from the confines of his now-dirtied tux. He unscrews the lid and takes a long swig, then holds the drink out to me.

I grab it and let the hot liquid pour down my throat. Because this whole situation needed alcohol like ten minutes ago. "Why are you even in here, Uncle? On what charges?"

He scoffs. "Thalius has convinced the council I took part in stealing the Moonlight Sword. As if I ever cared for such trinkets."

"And in this version of events, who does he imagine poisoned you?" I ask.

He chuckles. "Myself, apparently, in an attempt to feign my innocence."

"None of this makes sense," I say, taking another sip.

"It's a coup, darling. It doesn't need to make sense." He pauses. "However, if one was to retrieve the Moonlight Sword, the council may be forced into admitting they were wrong, on account of public pressure."

I nod, offering the bottle to Elias next. "So what sect are you?" I ask. "Lix Tetrax or the Unfettered?"

He takes a swig of the rum. "Lix Tetrax. But I suspect the White Rider seeks the First Vampire."

"You mean…"

He nods. "I believe the Dead Tree is the prison. And I am the key."

I snatch the bottle back. Yes, come to mommy. "And the First Vampire is trapped within. Waiting to start a massacre." Another sip. "So how do we stop the White Rider?" I ask. "Cause last I remember, he kicked both our asses."

"There is a way," says Elias. "The Shadow's Bane."

"The shadow's what now?"

"Three artifacts. A sword, a bow, and a cloak."

I frown. "Wait, you were actually serious about that at the party?"

He chuckles. "The Moonlight Sword is the first piece. I had hoped it would be enough on its own, but alas… you saw what happened."

I nod, drinking again, then pass the bottle to Sly.

He takes a moment to just breathe in the smell before taking a delicate sip. "Together, the items are said to make one a Master of Darkness," Sly says. "Together, they form the Shadow's Bane. They are: the Moonlight Sword. The Twilight Bow. And the Shadow Mantle."

I raise an eyebrow. "The Shadow Mantle? Like a mantelpiece?"

"No, a cloak," he says, exasperated. "Mantle is another word for cloak. Seriously, I can't believe young people these days."

Elias nods. "I know."

"Oh, I meant both of you," Sly says with a smirk.

The Prince scowls. "I am more than a century old."

Sly chuckles. "As I said, young people." He passes the bottle back to me.

"Well, we know where the sword is," I say.

"With the White Rider," adds Elias.

Sly nods. "Exactly, which is why you cannot face him head-on. You must fight him on your own terms. You must... discover his identity."

"Then I can reclaim the sword," says Elias, beaming.

"Then we can set a trap," I add, enjoying the makings of a kickass plan. "So, where are the other two pieces?"

Elias shrugs.

But Sly pauses, smiling coyly. "Pass me the bottle and I'll tell you." I hand it over it with no sadness whatsoever. Like totally none. "I haven't got a clue about the Shadow Mantle, otherwise called a cloak," he eyes me pointedly, "but the Twilight Bow is hidden within Crimson Castle."

"No," says Elias, lurching forward, his shackles yanking him back. "It can't be. It..."

"What's his deal?" I ask, pointing over my shoulder.

Sly grins. "The Crimson Castle is his home."

"And I'm not going back," says Elias, his voice quick and full of fire.

I shrug. "No problem. I'm going alone anyway."

"To an unknown world?" asks Sly skeptically. "It may help to take the prince along."

I try to speak as sweetly as possible. Emphasis on try. "Sure, I'll perhaps consider that when, you know, I actually escape." I grab the rum and hold it up to Elias in a mock toast. "So, Prince of Darkness, is this the part where you give me the whole join or die spiel? Now that I know the secret and everything?"

"No," he says softly. "Perhaps another will. But I will not."

Before I can reply, we are interrupted by a whisper coming from the door. "Psst. Iris..." That voice... I recognize that voice.

"Callie?" I jump to my feet and run up to the open grate.

Sure enough, she's there. My best friend, covered in a gray cloak and hood, white bandages peeking out around her collar.

"You're alive," I say, tears blurring my eyes.

"Thanks to you and Theo," she says with a small smile.

"Shut it. I'm the one who threw a dagger into you."

She shrugs. "I'm the one who tried to fight like a fool. I mean, in those heels? What was I thinking?"

We both chuckle. "I'm glad they didn't lock you up," I say.

"Well…" she chews on her lip. "They tried. They handcuffed me at the healers. But Nurse Betty helped me slip out when the watchers weren't looking. She doesn't like what's going on here one bit."

"So you came to bust us out, right?" I ask, jumping up and down, my blood already pumping for some sweet revenge.

She frowns. "Kinda. You see, I don't have the key."

"Oh."

"Yeah… but I did bring you something." She holds up a tray with bacon, grilled asparagus, and a cup of blood. "It's how I snuck down here."

I sigh. "So you're delivering our meal?"

She winks. "And something else too." She holds up the tray and slides it through the grate. Then whispers. "It's from a friend."

Metal clanks in the distance, and Callie's eyes grow panicked. "I need to go," she says hurriedly. "I'll be safe. Just get out of here." Without another word, she turns and runs away, disappearing in the shadows.

I step away from the door, glancing at the tray, Callie's words haunting me.

It's from a friend.

She meant not from her.

But what other friends do I have?

I move the bacon and asparagus aside, but the tray is empty underneath. I slide my fingers into the blood and—

Something bites my hand.

It burns.

Crawling up my skin.

Leeching onto my wrist.

Sly and Elias rush to my side, but there is nothing they can do.

Red lines etch themselves onto my skin.

My flesh singes and blisters.

I bite down on my tongue, drawing blood, my eyes shut with pain.

And then the agony fades.

The smoke dissipates.

The fire withers.

And only a mark is left.

A symbol burned into my skin.

Elias steps back. "A demon mark," he whispers.

And then I hear it. A voice in my head.

Hello, Iris. We have so much to talk about.

INFERNA

The voice is deep and thick, vibrating with power. *You are more important than you realize, First Hunter.*

"Um... who is this?"

That is of little consequence. All you need to know is that I have been watching you, Iris, and I think the two of us can benefit from a partnership. You see, we share a common foe. The White Rider.

Elias and Sly both look at me oddly. "What's going on, darling?" asks my uncle.

I shrug. "Oh, just talking to a voice in my head."

"That's impossible," says the prince. "A mark connects you with a demon. Allows them to sense your location. But mental communication is unheard of."

"A demon?" I ask. "So someone wants my soul or something?"

No, says the voice. *I only propose a bargain. We help each other.*

"Sure, creepy voice. I'll totally take you at your word."

I'm not lying.

"No offense, but for all I know, you're the White Rider himself. So..."

Understandable. I will demonstrate my use.

"Right..."

I will help you break free from this prison. The escape will start in three...

Wait.

Two...

Hold on.

One...

The frame of the cell door sparks and the giant piece of trimantium rips from its hinges, smashing to the ground. My shackles fall to the floor, unlocked. So do Elias's. "Oh, shit," I say, pointing at the open entryway.

Elias frowns, pointing at my skull. "Was that?"

"Yes. The voice." I pause. "Think it needs a name better than the voice though."

Names are inconsequential.

"I got it," I say. "Silence."

Are you implying something?

"Nope. Not a thing."

I point at Sly. "What about his shackles?"

His restraints block magic, says Silence. *I cannot remove them remotely.*

I see.

Sly scoots past us. "Perhaps we shouldn't dally, huh kids?"

He's right. Ten watchers are heading your way.

Okay then...

"Let's go," I take the lead, running up the dungeon stairs, Sly and Elias at my heels. "I need to get to Inferna. Find this Crimson Castle and Twilight Bow."

"Anxious to reach hell, are we?" asks Elias.

"Anxious to stop the White Rider."

"We'll need a mirror," says the prince.

"Thought you didn't want to go," I say.

"I don't. But I need the Twilight Bow. Besides, you could use my help."

"Pfft. You weren't much help against the rider."

He nods. "True. But I did distract him, giving you a chance to escape. Not my fault you stayed."

"Pro tip. The First Hunter doesn't run."

He smiles coyly. "Except for right now."

"Correct. Except for right now." I place my fingers in my mouth and whistle.

"Calling your pet manticore again?" asks Elias.

"Yep. And I'm not leaving Earth without him."

The prince faces Sly. "So where's the nearest mirror, old-timer?"

"Old-timer?" He grimaces. "One does not call an eternal being an old-timer." He combs his smooth hair back with his shackled hand. "Now that we have that clear. The closest mirror is in the first room to our left once we leave the dungeons. In the meanwhile, how about you cast an illusion over us."

"Kind of blew through my magic while sneaking into the dance," says Elias. "Need a little time to recover."

That reminds me. Renewal. It's back up. Yay. I get one free death this morning. Or night. Or… what time is it even?

"Ten watchers up ahead," I say, hearing their footsteps in the distance. Seems Silence wasn't lying.

Elias cracks his knuckles, grinning. "Wonderful."

"Easy, vampire. No unnecessary violence. Unless someone commits an illegal act, they're off the table."

"Your table perhaps. My table needs redecorating."

I palm my face, sighing. Vampires. Can't live with 'em. Can't… well, you know, my code prevents killing. Might be time to change some of the rules though.

The watchers are almost upon you, says Silence. *Wait. Something is wrong. Someone is ahead of them. Someone terrible. Someone—*

Oh, it's just Imenath.

He steps from the shadows, clad in his skeleton armor, wielding a spiked silver mace. "We meet again, hunter," he roars.

"Imenath, I really don't have time—"

"The eternal battle continues."

"No. No, it doesn't."

"Who shall prevail this time—"

"How are you even here, buddy?" I ask.

"Imenath heard Iris had been sent to dungeon. Imenath sought out his great foe. Blood will be spilled—"

"Look, Imenath," I wrap an arm over his shoulder. "We're kinda breaking out right now, and you're blowing our cover, man. We need—"

Footsteps. Metal clanging.

The watchers arrive, wielding swords and spears and daggers. Wait a second...

"Those are mine!" I yell, pointing at a petite Fae holding my babies.

She clutches them possessively and speaks in a high-pitched voice. "Surrender peacefully and—"

"The Hunter is mine," roars Imenath. "You shall not take her."

The watchers glance at one another in confusion. "Um... who are you again?" asks the small Fae.

Ouch. Wrong question.

Imenath roars with unbridled rage and passion. He charges into the watchers, spinning his mace overhead. "I am Imenath the Terrible. Number three on the most wanted list. And today, watchers, I shall be your doom."

No. Pretty sure he won't actually manage to hurt any of them. But this does make for a good distraction.

Imenath crashes into the watchers, knocking them down like bowling pins.

I rush forward, grabbing my precious daggers off the floor, then run past the watchers. Sly and Elias follow. The watchers try to keep up, but well... Imenath impresses me for once. I mean, check out that form. He must have really been working out in his spare time. I give him a thumbs up before leaving. I swear he sheds a tear.

"This room," yells Sly, taking the lead, heading for a pristine white door.

Only one problem.

Thalius.

He sprints down the stares, his fur cape drifting behind him, his silver-blue hair a mess. "Don't be fools," he spits, drawing his signature weapons. Two silver gauntlets, each with three claws extending from the knuckles. The Mittens of Justice.

I'm kidding. They're actually called The Ravagers. And they're a sweet package. Amazing craftsmanship. Legendary material. Don't mind me, just fangirling here for a second. For the claws. Not Thalius. So over that Fae.

I spin my daggers. "Step away from the door, Thalius."

He smiles one creepy ass smile. Then reaches under his cape and pulls out...

No.

He holds his claws up against the silver kitten. "Surrender, Iris. Or your manticore feels my sting."

He has Theo.

My baby.

My precious lion.

Oh, Thalius thinks he can mess with the First Hunter. But he is so wrong.

I wink at Theo.

He winks back.

Go time.

I toss my daggers straight at the keeper's face.

He holds Theo up as protection as we both knew he would, and my mighty kitten shifts, growing in size, ripping out of his grasp and falling, quickly shifting to travel size again as he hits the floor.

And my daggers hit Thalius in the—

Oh crap, he dodges.

My daggers impale the door as Theo jumps on my shoulder, hissing at our foe.

This may be a trickier fight than I thought.

Sly leans into my ear. "Go, my darling. I'll distract him."

"But—"

"But nothing. I'm the parental figure here," he says, standing tall. "Time I did something responsible. Besides, they won't kill me. Thalius would need the approval of the entire council for such a measure and he shall never have it, isn't that right, keeper?"

Thalius scowls, flashing his claws. "You're no match for me, old-timer."

"Old-timer," says Sly lowly. "Old-timer?" he growls. "Old-timer! Well, this old-timer is about to kick your ass, little boy!" He charges, swinging his manacles at Thalius.

The Fae dodges in a panic.

I hate to leave my uncle, but he's right. We need this distraction, because I'm sure more watchers are on the way, and I'd rather not fight people who are only trying to do their job. Most of us are kindred spirits, after all. So I dash for the room, pulling my daggers from the door and sheathing them in my belt. Now, time for...

"Where's the mirror?" I ask, glancing around, seeing a small room full of boxes.

Elias points at a table. "I believe it's there."

I follow his gaze to the— "No. No. Don't tell me that's the mirror you had shoved up your—"

"It may be," he says somberly. "It very well may be."

I wince, reaching for the coin-sized portal and, no I just can't. Okay, little bird? I can't.

Elias holds out his arm. "Hold my hand. I'll take the lead."

I take a deep breath, clutching his fingers. "Okay. Okay. I'm ready."

He nods. "I promise I'll be gentle."

Then he takes the mirror and swoosh. It's like I turn into a bunny being pulled from a hat. But instead of being pulled out it's more like I'm shoved in. Quickly and disturbingly and repeatedly until...

Poof.

I pop out the other side.

And step into hell. It looks like...

A beach?

Golden sand shifts under my boots. A light breeze drifts through the air. Warm sunlight falls down on... wait a second. Warm sunlight? Vampire?

Shit.

I rush to Elias, throwing my cape over him and—

He stands peacefully, eyes closed, bathing in the light, breathing deeply of the fresh air. "Oh, how I missed you, Inferna," he whispers.

I study him carefully from all angles. "Hold up. Why are you not a shish kebab right now?"

He smiles. "Only your Earth's sun harms vampires. Here, we are free to walk day and night."

A part of me still expects him to spontaneously combust. But he doesn't. So I guess we're good? Maybe? "Right," I say. "I remember reading that somewhere, but Sly has me reading things all the time. Suppose that's why vampires like it here so much, huh?"

Elias nods. "I heard it was even more popular when one was allowed blood slaves, not that I approve of the practice. It was before my time."

A few feet away, two men dressed in golden armor sit on wooden chairs, their legs propped up as they read from leather books. The closer man glances up from his entertainment and squints. "Marco, are you seeing what I'm seeing?"

His partner looks over at us. "It can't be... Roco, is that? Bloody hell, it's them." The two guards stand in unison, drawing their swords.

Elias steps forward, grinning. "Marco. Roco. My favorite guards, who served my mother so loyally. Let's talk about this—"

They point their weapons at him. "Sorry Prince," says Marco, "but we can't let you pass."

"You're wanted," explains Roco.

The prince nods nonchalantly. "Yes, of course. Number one on the most wanted list and all."

"No, you're not," says Marco, frowning. "Not anymore. She is." He points his finger at...

Well, me.

Elias raises an eyebrow. "Are you serious? That's preposterous. I've cultivated my reputation for years, carefully tailored my image, then she's accused of doing one thing wrong and suddenly she's number one? I mean, what's the Council of Hunters thinking?"

I shrug. "Sorry, I guess? But you know, First Hunter here."

Elias groans, throwing up his arms dramatically. "Please tell me I'm at least number two."

Marco shakes his head. "Sorry, Prince. But they say a silver lion beast thing is number two."

"A silver lion beast thing?" Elias's jaw drops as he glances over at Theo, sitting comfortably on my shoulder, cute little eyes closed. "You're ahead of me as well?"

Kitten Theo smiles.

The two guards exchange confused looks. "You mean, that's the killer beast monster?" asks Marco.

Roco sighs. "It's like I'm always saying, the list just isn't what it used to be."

Marco nods. "Yeah. Remember the gray beast?"

Roco smiles fondly. "Oh, how I miss those years. There used to be some real challenges for guards like us back in the day. Now it's all, sitting on the beach reading and guarding against kittens apparently."

"Youngsters don't know how easy they have it," finishes Marco.

I step forward, holding up my bare fists. "I can give you a real challenge, boys? Care to guess?"

"Fighting the First Hunter?" they ask together.

"Nope."

"Nope?"

I raise a finger. "Letting us pass, then having to hunt us down so you can fight the First Hunter."

They look at each other. "Suppose that *would* be difficult," says Marco.

"Could be fun," agrees Roco.

"But…"

"Nah," they finish in unison.

Marco points his sword at my chest. "Afraid we'd be fired for letting highly wanted criminals pass."

I nod. "Sure, but… why are you guys guarding this mirror again?"

Marco stands tall, pounding his armor over his heart. "Mirrors are a rare commodity in Inferna, you see. This being a world full of vampires, all portals must be carefully guarded, otherwise anyone could go anywhere, and what a security nightmare that would be."

Roco smacks his partner on the shoulder. "Why are you telling her? She's the enemy?"

"Innocent until proven guilty, I always say."

I nod sagely. "Sure, but why are *you* guarding this mirror? Certainly, two experienced and brave guards such as yourself have more important things to protect?"

Marco clears his throat. "Well, we used to but…"

"We failed," says Roco, his eyes turning red.

Elias frowns. "What happened?"

"It's… so horrible," whimpers Marco. "Can barely speak of it."

Elias sighs, glancing my way. "Can I knock them out, please?" he whispers.

I shake my head. "No unnecessary violence."

"Fine," he hisses, turning back to the guards and raising his voice. "Well, as much as I would like to keep chatting, we do have business to attend to. So take us to my parents. I will explain everything, and we can be on our way."

"But that's the thing," says Marco. "Your mother, the Queen, she's—"

"Missing," finishes Roco.

Elias blinks. "Missing? How?"

"No idea," cries Marco. "We were her royal guards, and we have no bloody clue."

"Disgraceful it is," adds Roco, wiping his eyes. "Queen Arianna deserved better than our lot. So that's why *we're* guarding this mirror. Only thing we're good for anymore."

Elias grabs them by the shoulders, his voice panicked. "What of my father?"

"He went looking for her as soon as it happened," says Marco. "Folk haven't seen him for months now."

"Who rules in their stead?"

"It's been every realm for themselves," says Roco.

You're wasting time, says Silence. *The vampire king and queen are inconsequential.*

"Could be related to the White Rider," I whisper. "He seems to have a thing for royal blood."

Either way, you must make haste to the castle and—

The wooden chairs explode. Sand sprays into the sky.

"Bloody hell," roars Marco. He pulls out a spyglass, you know, the thing pirates use, and holds it up to his eye to scan the water. I follow his gaze, seeing a dark ship out on the waters.

"Damn raiders," curses Roco.

Something flies from the ship.

A cannonball.

This one shoots over our heads.

Right into a wall of stone. Right into a...

"Shit. That's a castle," I say, pointing behind me. "Is that our destination?"

"No," hisses Elias. "That's High Castle. Seat of the High King and Queen. Or at least it was."

High Castle, huh? Pretty dandy, I must say. The fortress towers over the land, taking up the better part of an island. The white walls sparkle in the sun like some fairytale Disney logo. Banners of all colors hang from the towers, drifting in the wind. Pride supporters, maybe? I can get down with that. A massive stone bridge connects two sections of the castle, covered in emerald ivy. Red flowers cling to the vines. There's room enough for probably like one hundred kitchens. Personally, I could get used to a place like this. Yes, I can see it already. My belongings can go into the main hall. I can go on a shopping spree for the rest. And—

Another cannonball hits the bridge.

"How dare they fire at my precious castle!" I roar.

Elias frowns. "*Your* castle?"

"Yes. I have vowed to be its protector."

"When?"

"Just now in my mind."

His incredulous expression is interrupted by the blow of a battle horn from beyond the walls. Soldiers dressed in red and green storm onto the battlements. Archers take their positions. Though they are too far to fire on the ship, they could stop a landing party. People scream and yell in the distance. A group of vampires further away leaves the beach, rushing for the safety of the castle gates.

"Something's wrong," says Elias, staring at the soldiers manning the defenses. "Those aren't my family's colors. Marco, Roco, what happened?"

They shrug. "We aren't privy to much anymore, my Prince," says Marco.

"Been here protecting the mirror," adds Roco.

Another cannonball hits the battlements, tearing into the stone, sending two archers flying and screaming as they fall to their deaths.

Okay. That's it. I need to do something before more lives are taken. I turn to the guards. "These raiders are committing an illegal act by attacking High Castle, correct?"

They both nod. "Yes. Highly illegal," says Marco.

"Thought so." I nod at Theo. "Let's do this, buddy."

He leaps off my shoulder, growing to full size, his wings unfurling over the beach, launching sand into the air.

Roco's jaw drops. "It's the silver lion beast thing!"

"It flies!" yells Marco. "No one said it could fly!"

"It's unstoppable!"

I jump on Theo's back, grabbing onto his blue mane. Elias lands behind me, wrapping his arms around my waist.

I nudge him with my shoulder. "You *could* hold onto his fur."

He grins. "But this is so much more fun."

His hands do feel comforting, I suppose. They're so strong and graceful and nimble—

Cut it out, Iris. It's just that trick he has for making you think things. He—

Elias pulls his hands away, clutching the fur. "Of course, I wouldn't want to make you uncomfortable, love."

Huh, didn't see that coming. Well...

Time to fly.

We dash into the sky, drifting over clear sapphire waters, small boats dotting the waves below. The raider ship grows closer, its white sails glittering in the light. It's kind of old-school, like a real pirate vessel, with a hull made from auburn wood filled with gun ports, (basically special holes crammed with cannons) and a black flag waving in the wind. But it's kind of new-school too, with crazy sails I've never seen before that remind me of fins, and a mechanism of golden pipes lining the side of the craft. Clocks hang in seemingly random locations. The masthead is a scantily clad, ample-bosomed woman who seems to stare at me from all angles. Wait... Did she just wink? I swear she just winked. Okay, whoever designed this ship is a freaking mad genius, because this thing is awesome.

It fires another cannonball. This one... uh oh, this one seems aimed at us. They probably think we're the High Castle defense team or something. Theo spins out of the way. That's right, suckers. You've got nothing on my manticore.

"Not that I mind a good fight," says Elias, eyeing the ship, "but don't we have more important matters to deal with? Like say, finding the Twilight Bow and stopping the White Rider?""

"I'm the First Hunter," I say, gritting my teeth. "Stopping criminals is my job." And in all honesty, between you and me, little bird, after holding back with the watchers and hunters, my hands are itching for a fight. Nothing like a good battle to blow off some steam.

But there's also another reason. Possibly the most important. "Listen, if there's a faction of vampires seeking to massacre all the worlds, I need to investigate them. And something tells me this ship is related, considering it's attacking your seat of government and all."

Elias nods. "Very well. But be careful, Iris."

I grin at him. "Don't worry, Prince. There are only three things I fear, and none of them are on that ship."

We reach our destination, hovering over the vessel. Dozens of men and woman run around below, scrambling for weapons. Only one stands still. A woman clad in black. Her silver hair braided on one side, wild and free on the other. Her eyes a deep emerald. She wears a pointy captain hat and holds an elegant rapier. She's their leader. My enemy.

"Hey Silence," I whisper. "Ready to help us fight? Maybe blow up some cannons like you blew up that door."

I drained the last of my powers helping you escape, says Silence. *It will be a long time before I can exert such strength again.*

Lovely...

I raise my daggers, ready to jump and dispense justice in the name of High Castle.

"Wait," says Elias, grabbing my shoulder, his eyes fixed on the woman with silver hair.

"Why?" I ask.

He sighs. "Because that's my sister."

AYA

*F*ull name: Aya'zee Vane Spero

Classification: Half Vampire / Half Fae

Title: High Princess of Hell

Physical Description: Five feet and a half, lithe, toned, green eyes, silver hair

Keeper and part of the Council of Hunters, representing the vampires.

May or may not be responsible for the coup against the Black Lotus.

But Iris, if she's a council member, why didn't you recognize her sooner? Because, little bird, I've only ever seen her in passing, never officially met her, and she looks different than she does on her poster. That way famous people sometimes look different in real life. A little less pristine. A little more gritty. Less Photoshopped.

So the question is... are we still fighting? I'm a little confused actually.

"Halt!" yells Aya'zee, gesturing to her crew. "Stand down."

They lower their weapons and step away from the cannons. Good sign, right?

"Can we trust her?" I ask Elias quietly.

"Not sure. Hmm… let me see." He cups his hands around his mouth and hollers down below. "My dear sister, can we trust you?"

"Depends," she yells back, still holding her rapier. "Are you working with Salez?"

Elias and I exchange a confused glance. "Don't think so," he says. "Why?"

Aya'zee finally sheaths her sword. "She's taken over High Castle."

"What?" roars Elias. He taps my shoulder fervently. "Take us down."

I nod, signaling Theo to land. I keep my daggers ready though. This could still be a trap. My lion thinks so too. He keeps his claws out, watching the crew for any sudden movements.

Elias hops off before we even touch the deck, running to his sister. "I heard mother and father are missing," he says. "They must just be on a secret mission or—"

Aya'zee shakes her head. "No mission, brother. They're missing. And the Seven Realms have gone mad in their absence. There are uprisings and rebellions everywhere. Just two days ago, I received word Salez and her supporters had captured High Castle. That's why I'm here. To take it back."

She gestures to the crew, and they resume their duties, firing cannonballs at the walls once more, scrambling to move the ship closer to shore. She walks the deck, surveying their work, yelling out commands from time to time like 'hoist anchor', 'lower the sails', 'prepare the arrows'. You know, sea captain things.

I step beside her and Elias, holding out my hand in greeting, trying to appear as dignified as possible because hey, at the end of this, I still want a promotion. "A pleasure to finally meet you, Aya'zee."

She clasps my hand, talking as we walk. "First, call me Aya. And second, the pleasure is all mine, Iris."

"You know me?" I beam.

She chuckles. "What kind of keeper would I be if I didn't keep tabs on the First Hunter?" She pauses. "Though, I suppose you're an ex-hunter now, on account of being wanted and all."

"We were framed," I say quickly, as Theo hops behind me, still full-size, still ready to protect me with all his being.

Aya rubs her magnificent pale chin. Seriously, her skin is smooth as cream and white as ivory. I kind of want touch it... but I shouldn't. I mean... I shouldn't, right?

What the hell is going on? Is she making me go crazy like her brother? Keep it together, Iris. Keep it together.

But that silver hair...

Argh. Focus.

"Innocent people don't usually escape from dungeons," says Aya, eyeing me skeptically.

Hopefully not because I'm doing anything weird, like salivating. I'm not, right? You'd tell me if I was, wouldn't you? I clear my throat, using my professional voice. "Well, no people usually escape from dungeons, so..."

"Fair point." She grins, flicking up her captain's hat. "To be honest, I like the both of you. One of you is tall, dark and stylish, and the other is, well, my brother." She gives me a wink.

Hold up now... is the Princess of Hell hitting on me?

I mean, my boat doesn't float down that stream, if you know what I mean, but if anyone could steer me in a different direction, I guess it'd be—

Snap out of it, Iris.

Aya chuckles, as if she can read my mind. "Technically, as per the vote of the council, I should arrest you, but I voted against your capture, so how about we do this instead: You help me retake High Castle, and I help you get wherever you're going."

Elias frowns. "Kind offer, but we do have a fairly large bounty on our heads. Your crew may let our whereabouts slip in order to—"

"Never," she says plainly. "My crew would rather die than betray my command." They puff up with pride as she speaks, and I see in their faces her words are true. Well, likely true. I suppose some of the crew could just be good at acting. At any rate...

"So let me get this straight," I say, pacing. "The real criminals are in High Castle, correct?" Because like, I was really hoping to be fighting by now.

"Yes," says Aya. "Salez is a lesser noble with grand aspirations. When the High Queen went missing, she gathered her forces and ventured south, raiding every village in her way, recruiting more supporters. Now, she sits on the throne, fancying herself ruler of the Seven Realms."

"That power grabbing piece of filth," spits Elias. "Didn't her brother try something similar years ago?"

Aya nods, her eyes distant. "Salazar. Our father would tell the story often." She pauses, smiling fondly. Then her smile fades, replaced by a cold, hard scowl. "But right now, Father is gone, and it's up to us to protect the people. So... are you with me?"

I hold up my hands. "Look, I like protecting the people and all that. But I thought this would just be a quick ass kicking. Now, it's all like, for our father, for the realms, a bit too political for my taste, personally. So I'm thinking, we just hop back on my manticore, and leave this business to you, beautiful person."

She scoffs. "Everyone in the Seven Realms is after you. Tell me, what kind of warlord couldn't use the gold promised for your capture?"

"Um... the nice kind?"

The crew doesn't seem to like my answer. A handful of them step closer, hands on their hilts. Aya gives them a stern glare and they pull back. "If you travel by sky," she continues, "you will be hunted day and night." She points at her brother. "I don't care if you have illusion. Any half-trained Fae will see through your tricks. What you need is discretion. What you need is my ship. The Dread Shark. Fastest vessel in Inferna."

She does make a good point.

"And remember," Aya says. "If you help me, you'll be taking down a tyrant. A petty dictator. But one who is not to be trifled with. One who will keep pillaging and murdering if not stopped right here, right now. Leave her be, and Salez will make even more allies. She already works with a group called the Unfettered."

The Unfettered, huh? The group seeking the First Vampire and eternal darkness? Elias and I exchange a meaningful look. "What have you heard about them?" I ask.

Aya grabs a spyglass and aims it at the castle. "Only that they seem to like stirring up trouble. If you believe the rumors, and I rarely do, they've been spreading dissent throughout the realms. Meeting in secret. Fueling hate. Supplying the revolts."

Well, well, this just got more interesting. If Salez is truly working with the Unfettered, then we need to have a little chat, woman to woman. She may have information about the rider's identity, and I need that info ASAP.

"Okay," I say, clutching my dagger tightly. "I'm in."

Aya grins devilishly. "Very well. I have a small army moving in on land. I need you to—"

I jump on Theo and aim him straight for the castle, my cloak whipping in the wind. Aya may have a plan, but I have my own. It's called decimation. Or maybe Iris and the High Castle. Or maybe… ah, who cares. Let's do this.

Queue epic soundtrack.

Dun… Dun… Dun Dun Dun… Dun…

Archers fire my way.

Theo evades, spiraling through the sky.

I kiss the top of his head for luck then jump off, diving toward the fortifications, gaining momentum as I fall.

The vampire soldiers, about two dozen of them, gawk at me like I'm crazy.

"That's Iris," one of them yells. *"Iris?" "Yeah, the First Hunter." "They say she poisoned her own uncle." "They say she moves like the devil himself."*

I land amongst them, wielding my daggers like a master, tearing past their defenses. Half of them flee immediately, the other half I disarm in an instant. Poor vamps. None of them are over level five. Their movements feel like slow motion to me.

I rush into the castle, disarming anyone in my way like…

Bam.

Swoosh.

Kaboom.

And... oh my, the castle's even prettier on the inside. Tapestries depicting great battles hang on every wall. Green vines interwoven with purple flowers fall from the ceiling. Soft aromas drift through the air. It is a little damp though, and lonely. If it were up to me, I would decree immediately, one kitten in every room. Kittens for everyone!

Oh right, the battle. I fight my way to the throne room. Security isn't all that tight, actually. Only a few dozen guards, half of whom run away.

As I near the center of the fortress, a foul stench fills the air and crimson stains begin to cover the floors. Corpses hang, pinned to the walls, their eyes cut out. A warning from a conqueror.

I kick open a giant door, entering the main hall. It's a massive room with many windows, bathing the walls with golden light. A red carpet runs along the floor. A giant crystal chandelier hangs from the ceiling. And at the end of the room stand two thrones. Ancient things carved from black marble, etched with symbols of both Fae and vampire. Seats of the High King and Queen of Inferna. But today, one chair is empty. On the other sits a frail woman, her skin pale and sunken. She clutches a sword far too big for her hands and wears a black fur coat more suited to comfort than combat. She seems no conqueror—except for her eyes. They are quick and fierce, like lightning waiting to strike.

"Salez," I say, pointing my dagger forward. "Lay down your sword and surrender the castle to its rightful heir, Aya'zee Vane Spero."

Salez chews on her lip, then spits at my feet. A big wad of icky goop. "So the Dread Princess sent you, did she? Very well. Make it quick, First Hunter. I won't die begging." She holds out her neck, staring at me.

Except I don't kill people. Didn't anyone get the memo about that? Sheesh. "Tell me about the White Rider," I command, walking forward, closing the distance between us.

"The story?"

"You know he's no story," I hiss.

She chuckles. "Can he not be both? Story and man?"

"You mean he's actually the creature?" I ask. "The creature from legends?"

She laughs, and her laugh turns into a cough. "You think you're on the right side, don't you? Fighting for the High Queen and King? The rightful rulers? But hear this... you have all been deceived. The King and Queen have a secret. They thought they could hide their misdeed from the people, but instead it festered, growing like a cancer. I have learned the truth. The rider told me. He is the reckoning to come. And now, Inferna will suffer the sins of its rulers. Suffer so it can be born anew."

"What secret?" I growl.

She laughs again.

"Who is the White Rider?"

Her cackle turns into a cough. "You are a pawn, girl. You do not even see the game being played. You—"

"Who is he?" I roar, and something snaps inside me. An energy fills my bones, and I grab her by the collar, lifting her into the air.

She freezes, scanning my eyes. "Perhaps not a pawn," she says softly. "But a queen. Very well, I will tell you—"

An arrow strikes through her neck.

Blood spurts from her mouth.

I drop Salez and scan the windows. Whoever shot her is already gone. When I return my attention to the woman, she is dead, her windpipe broken, her eyes staring blankly at the sky.

I close them, whispering a hunter's prayer for her soul, then set out searching the castle. There is nothing out of the ordinary to find, and soon enough Aya's troops secure the fortress. As the sun begins to set, I return to the Dread Shark with Theo.

"Are you hurt?" Elias asks tenderly, his eyes fixed on the blood covering my cloak.

"Not mine," I say simply, leaning against the mast, my mind numb.

Aya and a dozen of her crew drink from large tankards overflowing with foam, cheering and toasting to victory. When the princess sees me, she saunters over, grinning with charm. "Iris," she says merrily. "The conquering hero."

I don't return her smile. I don't feel like a hero.

She sighs, patting my shoulder. "I too would be more like you right now if I didn't have to put on a show for the crew. But they need to know what they did today was right. They need to know they can kill and still feel happiness afterwards. Because in the end, they will need to do this again." She pauses. "Just remember, thanks to you the castle has been taken with minimal casualties. Be proud of that, at least. Don't let the misery swallow you whole."

I take a deep breath, trying to calm the nerves within. "Just... hold up your end of the bargain."

"Right. About that..." Aya draws her rapier, aiming it at my throat. "The council sends their regards."

INTERLUDE

Written by Elias Vane Spero
Illustrated by Elias Vane Spero
The Prince of Darkness Comes Home

A meditation on immortality and morality.
A vampire's lament.

THAT'S IT. I'm writing myself into the narrative. It's all been Iris this, Iris that. It's time to focus the story on what really matters.

Me.

Elias Vane Spero.

I've been number one on the most wanted list for years. I've searched for the Moonlight Sword for decades. It's *my* blood the Whiter Rider wants. Clearly, *I* am the true star of this book. The most interesting person on the page. The *pièce de résistance*, as it were.

What's that, good fellow?

You want to get back to Iris? Want to see what happens after my sister pulls a blade on the once First Hunter?

All pish posh really. Insignificant.

What really matters is me. What I've been up to. You see, while Iris was off taking over a castle, quite splendidly I might add, I was scouring the ship known as the Dread Shark, looking for clues as to my sister's true intentions. Yes, I may have found a flask along the way, and yes, perhaps I borrowed this black wool cloak and leather vest without asking, as well as acquired a few more peculiar items, but the point is...

I found some correspondence between Aya and the council. Seems my dear sister has been busy writing letters to Thalius of a particular devious nature. The two are scheming, it appears, though their exact plan is hard to decipher. The main details I can gather are...

One: Aya was at the Black Lotus during the time Sly was poisoned.

Two: Thalius knows Iris and I are on the Dread Shark.

So, when my dear sister points a rapier at Iris' throat, I am in no way surprised. She may be a Spero, but she's also a Vane. Betrayal runs in our blood.

Of course, I have prepared for just such an occasion. Drawing my sword, a pitiful thing I grabbed back at the Lotus, I point my blade at Aya. "What is the meaning of this?" I roar, dramatically. I must sell my surprise, after all.

My sister scoffs. "It was fun using you to retake High Castle, but it's time you returned to your cell."

Her crew, a mismatched lot of men and women who look pulled from the darkest of alleys, cheer and holler and grin, drawing their crude blades. This is what they wanted from the start. The bounty on our heads. They only postponed our capture so Iris could help them win the battle. Clever lot, though of course it was Aya's idea from the start.

Iris looks mad as hell, her brow pinched in the most delightful manner. "You used me."

"For a good cause," says the princess. "Now, if you'd be so kind as to follow me to the brig below." Her crew closes in as if to say, *or else*.

At least, they try to close in.

One of them, a large man wearing a white shirt that is much too tight, (seriously, where is a proper tailor when you need one?) collapses forward, his knees hitting the floor with a hard thunk, his tankard spilling over the deck. The woman to his side falls next, clutching her stomach. The young fellow behind her stumbles, walking into the mast and knocking himself unconscious. One by one, the rest of the crew follows, falling into a deep slumber.

I would feign surprise, but there's no need at this point.

Aya clutches her stomach, grimacing. "You... you drugged the rum."

I told you I was prepared, did I not, good fellow?

"Yes, dear sister," I say, sheathing the sword I never intended to use.

"Where'd you get the poison?" she asks, her knees trembling under her weight.

"From your own personal stock, of course," I say, smirking, stepping forward until our faces are only inches apart. "It was quite simple to sneak into your private cabin, acquire the goods, then sneak below deck and... shall we say, season the casks of rum. You're getting rusty, my dear." I pat her cheek as her eyes begin to close.

"I suppose... this still works with my plan," she says, her voice thick.

Iris twirls her daggers, Theo growling at her back. "Your plan to turn us over to Thalius?"

The princess chuckles. "I was going to set you free, numbskulls."

"Right," Iris says sarcastically, "And I was going to bake you a cake that said: Thank you for betraying us. Not!"

"Oh, she's telling the truth," I say with the charm that comes so easily to me. "Aya was going to set us free."

The princess furrows her brow. "You knew? Then why..."

"I had to drug the all the casks, dear sister. Of course, I could have tipped you off before you drank the rum. But I still owe you one for that time you stole my pants."

She laughs at the memory. "The castle maids didn't seem to mind."

"No, I suppose they didn't," I say, recalling my youth with fondness.

Iris shakes her head. "I'm confused. If you were going to set us free, why the charade? You said this crew would rather die than betray you."

"Are you kidding me?" Aya chuckles. "They're just some mercenaries I picked up on my journey. I just said that to keep them in line. They'd tie me to the anchor if they actually thought I would let you go. I convinced them I would manipulate you into helping us take the castle, then lock you in our brig. In reality, I would let you escape by a small boat and..." She pauses, slipping down to her knees. "But I suppose this is even better, huh? This way, no one can say I was privy to your escape. Well played, brother."

I perform an elegant bow. It is always good to receive appreciation where appreciation is due.

Iris puts her hands on her hips. "So what, when she wakes up she can 'pretend' to try and hunt us down for the council?"

I raise my hand. "Exactly, and while she's pretending to search for us, Thalius and his ilk will focus on other matters." I pause, studying my sister who I have not seen for so long, laying there against the mast, her face so peaceful. "Do not be mistaken, hunter. Aya is no pawn. If she is corresponding with the council, she is playing them without their knowledge. She always likes to hold the strings, my sister does. That is how I know she won't betray us."

The Dread Princess smirks. "You know me well, brother."

I hold her face gently as she slides to the floor. "Rest now, dear sister. I hope to see you soon."

Her eyes mist. "You've been too long gone, Elias." There is a pause as both of us consider what my choices have cost our family, but it is short-lived, given she's about to pass out and still has words on her tongue. "Head below deck. Pull a lantern at the back of the ship, third level. There you will find your boat." She smirks, and finally her eyes close as she falls asleep.

"Now," I say, standing and admiring my handy work—as in all the people passed out on the ship. "Time to go." I make my way below deck, stepping over all manner of unconscious filth. Near the back of the Dread Shark, with some careful observation, I discover the appropriate lantern, pull and… lo and behold, a secret door opens, and there is our escape vessel, a small boat packed with food, packets of blood, a map of Inferna, and extra furs for the cold.

"See," I say, untying the boat and preparing to lower it into the water through an open hatch below. "Aya spoke the truth."

Iris crosses her arms, a kitten size Theo perching on her shoulder. She pouts her lip in that endearing way. "Sure. Or she's just playing you."

"Perhaps," I say, as we both climb into the too-small vessel. We're quite pinched for space, our knees almost touching as we sit facing each other. I use a pulley system to lower us to the waves. There are a pair of paddles onboard for emergencies, but we won't be needing them. I wave my hand, and voila, the boat begins to glide through the dark waters on its own, making good time.

Can Iris do that, good fellow?

No. She cannot. And now you are beginning to understand the true protagonist of this tale.

"Impressive," says the hunter, leaning back against the front of the boat, resting her head on a bundle of furs, Theo cuddling under her arm. She stares at the stars and the three moons of my homeland.

"The perks of being a Shade," I say modestly. "The magic of the Fae, the strength of the vampire. And of course, the downsides of both."

"Like no fun in the Earth sun?" she asks playfully.

"And a lust for blood," I add. "And of course, there's my unnatural good looks and attraction."

"That's a downside?" she asks, familiar skepticism on her beautiful face.

I nod somberly. "Even a gift can be a curse, Iris. Everyone, no matter how kind and pure, sees me as an object first, a person second. No matter how hard I try, I cannot stop the effect I have on others. The way they unnaturally crave me, the way they need my body above all else."

I expect her to laugh. Most do when they hear my side of the tale. But instead she tilts her head to the side, quietly considering my words. "It was intense at first," she says slowly. "This supernatural power you have over others. But the more time I spend with you, the less it seems to affect me." She pauses. "Perhaps I'm developing an immunity."

I sigh, having heard this part before. "As if to a poison."

She shakes her head, eyes thoughtful. "As if to myself."

I blink, startled by her response.

"After all," she continues, "It's my own emotional response that's overstimulated. My own cravings that cloud my mind. The more time I spend with you, the more control I develop over my own self." She shrugs casually. "At least, I'd like to think so, anyway."

She prefers to carry the blame?

Others are always eager to throw it upon me. But not this woman. I find it both odd and comforting. Both strange and seductive at once.

For the first time, I feel like sharing more than pulling back. "Have you been to Inferna before?" I ask.

"Yes," she says with a yawn, "but only very briefly, to catch a mark. I didn't venture far."

She's tired, I realize. Falling asleep. My kind doesn't require rest as often as humans, so sometimes I forget how much the needs of their fragile bodies dictate their schedule.

"Tell me about your home," she says quietly, her eyes closing.

I unroll the leather map of Inferna. Not for her benefit. But for my own. Not to remind myself of the locations, those I have burned into my mind. But to gaze upon the shape of my world, to feel the fabric and imagine it is the good dark earth I once called my own.

I spread my hands over the map, pointing from place to place, talking as I do. From time to time, Iris tilts her head my way, letting me know she still listens. I tell her of Inferna. How it is made of seven realms. Seven rings that spiral around each other. In the center lies High Castle. From there, canals run in all directions.

North—

South—

East—

West—

Connecting all corners of the world. Unifying lands as varied and diverse as their people. The Seven Realms, each named after one of the deadly sins.

Each named after one of Lucian's sons. The original Princes of Hell.

The first ring of land, the one we are entering now, is the realm of greed. Though it is dark, I can make out the marketplace where I would purchase trinkets with money I saved up chopping wood for my father. Past the sand dunes I can see the great cathedral built of sandstone, where I would climb too high and fall too far. Once, before I was born, my Uncle Niam, Prince of Greed, ruled this land. But he was, I am told, a vile man who cared for nothing but gold and slaves, and for his sins, he perished during the Midnight War. The great conflict that finally brought peace between vampire and Fae. Now my sister, Aya, rules the land, managing the finances of the Seven Realms when she finds the time.

The desert fades, making way for tropical trees and lush, vibrant plants. We are entering the realm of Lust. The place that never sleeps. Here, deep rhythmic music plays through the night, as scantily clad woman draped in silver and gold drink wine by the beach, and others swim naked in the water, yelling and howling to the moons. The men join them, their oiled muscles glistening under the burning lights of torches. For many years, I wasn't allowed in this realm of pleasure and decadence. But that doesn't mean I didn't sneak off, playing cards with Uncle Dean, Prince of Lust and ruler of this realm, as he taught me the ways of the world. This realm hides secrets of more substance than the self-indulgence on display, for my uncle is also a collector of artifacts and mysteries. No one knows the ancient world like him.

The fragrant smell of perfumes dwindles in the wind, replaced by the smell of fire and oil and fumes. And so we come to the third ring. The realm of Sloth, where tinkerers work day and night to bring marvelous inventions to life. They are lead by the greatest mind in our world, Uncle Ace, Prince of Sloth, the man who taught me how to build my first paper boat. I like to imagine he is there now, working on a new project to ease the lives of others. He is the reason people in Inferna say, "If you want something done fast, leave it to a lazy person."

The water turns harsher, the wind colder, for the further you travel from the center of Inferna, the more the heat and dryness fade away, replaced by fresh air and a bitter chill. We have come upon the realm of Gluttony, where my Uncle Zeb cultivates most of the food for the entire kingdom, throwing splendid feasts as fishermen sail dangerous waters, making sure to avoid the dark cliffs that dot this land.

The waters calm. The wind settles. And snow begins to fall from the sky, dotting my dark cloak with its gentle touch. We have come to the realm of Envy. Beyond here is still the realm of Pride, with its pristine white towers and purple banners, and further out lies the realm of War, a wild and untamed land my father hails from, and where he and my mother first fell in love. Aya and I often snuck out to the woods as children to practice our hunting and wilderness survival. We thought ourselves so clever, never realizing that my father's wolf, Baron, was not there as a furry pet, but as protector and ambassador for our parents. We weren't nearly as smart as we imagined.

Further still are the Outlands, a place yet unclaimed by the kingdom, and a place even Aya and I dared not venture in our youthful adventures. That is the true wild, where the laws of Inferna and its sister kingdom Avakiri do not apply. Where my parents' rule never extended. Where vampire, Fae and Shade live in lawlessness, forever at war with each other and themselves.

But we will go no further tonight. For the realm of Envy is my realm. It is where we shall find the Crimson Castle. The home I abandoned long ago.

A wolf howls in the distance, a sound so faint it does not stir Iris or Theo from their sleep. But I look to the moons and listen, basking in the sounds of the night I cherished as a child. Something stirs at the corner of my eye, and I follow the movement to its source.

A white wolf stands on the frozen shore, gazing at me with piercing blue eyes. It is larger than any beast of its kind should be, its claws large enough to tear a man in two. It can't be... but I would know that wolf anywhere. I remember running with him through the gardens at High Castle, playing fetch by the beach, following the beast as it followed my father, always by his side, the two of them inseparable, except when he acted as guard and babysitter to Aya and me.

"Baron?" I whisper.

The wolf tilts his head, then walks toward the forest, where dark trees cover the snow in shadow.

"Wait," I yell.

But he doesn't.

I spell the boat to reach the shore and jump onto the land, the earth crunching beneath my boots. I do not wish to wake Iris on a simple whim, but I cannot leave her and Theo undefended, so I clasp my hands together and whisper the words of the ancient Fae, summoning wards around our vessel. If any danger draws near, they will wake the hunter and the manticore, as well as alert me. With my protections in place, I rush into the forest, following the wolf prints in the snow.

It's not long before I reach my destination. A cave in the forest, shielded from the blizzard that is beginning to form. The white wolf, Baron, stands outside, glancing toward me with pleading eyes. Up close, I see he is injured, red marks spreading down his belly. He must have fought another beast. Something much larger and more powerful than even him.

I follow the wolf inside the cave, my enhanced vision allowing me to see in the darkness. We don't have to travel far, for the space is small, a cozy den of stone and leaves. In the pitch-black something stirs.

"Father?" I whisper.

Hoping he is by his wolf once again.

But my father is not here.

Instead, Baron stands over a massive corpse, whimpering and whining. It is another wolf, I realize. A female. His mate.

And she is dead.

Killed by the creature that attacked them.

But why bring me here, Baron? There is nothing I can do for her.

He nudges my hand with his wet nose, beckoning me closer. I crouch down, studying the large she-wolf, and then I see movement.

Near her belly, snuggling against her fur, lies a young pup, its coat black as night. The wolfling whines when he sees me, clinging to his mother.

"It's okay," I whisper, taking the pup into my arms. It is a boy, I realize. He is much too small, his body malnourished and weak, but still he finds the energy to lick my palm, his blue eyes meeting mine.

Baron rubs his head against that of his son's.

"This is why you called me, isn't it, boy?" I ask.

The great wolf simply tilts his head, then lies down by his mate, wrapping his tail around hers. His wounds are too great, I realize. He would not have been able to keep the pup safe. And with one final, heaving breath, the white wolf grows still, his life leaving him.

My heart clutches as grief strikes. But I know he will return. For Baron is a Spirit of these lands. A creature of the earth. I pet him as he fades, whispering sounds of comfort, and the giant wolf turns to ash under my hands, drifting away in the wind.

"See you soon, boy," I say, looking toward the moons, hoping he will find my father again. Hoping I will find them both.

Something growls behind the trees, branches snapping beneath its weight as it prowls closer. It seems the beast picked up my scent and returned for more prey. It comes slowly. An Akula, a monster three times my size, its breath fogging, its teeth dripping with blood. The creature has the body of a massive bear and the head of lion and it wears no skin, its muscles and bones exposed to the elements. When it rears back on its two hind legs, it towers over me, its slimy tongue wagging in the cold, bitter wind.

I clutch the wolf pup close to my chest, staring the beast in the eyes. "You should never have returned," I say, baring my teeth. "This pup is mine."

The Akula charges, falling upon me with its claws. I place the wolf behind me on the ground, protecting it with my own body. The beast tears at my back, ripping my cloak to shreds, peeling my flesh from my bones. I roar through the pain and throw myself upon the creature, fighting with my bare hands, biting into its neck, aiming for its jugular. I do not know how long we struggle, but in the end, I am drenched in blood, my head feverish, my muscles on fire, as I stand over the dead predator, red snow pooling at my feet. There is a sadness in me for felling such a great beast. But I warned him.

This pup is mine.

The wolfling runs into my arms, squirming and pleading. I whisper into his ears a song my parents would whisper to me, and I hold him close as I walk into the night, wondering where my father and mother have gone. And if I will find them alive.

Or like Baron and his mate, in the clutches of death.

DUKE

J'm back. Your girl Iris is in the house. Sorry for that interruption, by the way. Elias seems to have inserted some pages into the middle of my tale. Cheeky bastard. Time to continue the story that really matters.

Mine.

Oh, and I have to take a massive dump by the way. Just huge. So look away, little bird. Look away...

There. All better. Except...

Seems Aya forgot to pack toilet paper on the escape vessel. Very well, a leaf shall do. Maybe two. Maybe three. It was enormous, okay?

I'm almost done, so stress not, little bird. And don't act so disgusted. You do the same thing when you wake up from a long slumber, admit it. Though, hopefully you have access to softer tissue for your tush. At any rate, I shouldn't have to hide these things from you. We're friends, aren't we? Just gotta keep shit real here. (Did you catch the pun? Yeah, you did!)

I'm just glad Elias isn't around for this one. It's a stinker.

Speaking of... where is he?

I pull up my pants, looking around. Aha. Tracks!

Wolf prints. Unnaturally large wolf prints. And boots. Only one pair. Elias.

Did he go hunting?

I consider following him, but eh. I change my mind. The Prince of Darkness can handle a little hunt, and I'm not eating raw meat, so how about I build a fire. Takes only a moment to gather the logs and find a location protected from the growing blizzard. A circle of massive stones, reaching into the sky.

I arrange the sticks in a pyramid.

Theo helps, and by helps I mean oversees my work as he lies on a patch of snow, grinning. I swear he's thinking, 'Faster human. Faster!"

I pull a lighter from my cloak, and—

Wait. That's not a lighter. That's a piece of flint.

Hmm. Seems Inferna is anti-technology, like the Black Lotus, but even worse. Like, it replaced my lighter with a rock. I wonder what it did to my cellphone—

Oh shit, it's a leather journal with my contacts written out. Are you kidding me? Where are my apps? My games? I'm gonna lose my daily bonus check-in. Damnit.

Not cool Inferna, not cool. No wonder people call this place hell.

I strike my dagger against the flint, forming sparks to start the fire. Theo scoots closer, cuddling up on my lap as we watch the flames dance in the night. Minutes pass. And with so much quiet, my mind wanders. To Sly, back in the dungeons. To Callie, on the run somewhere. To food. Man, I'm starving. Why isn't Elias back yet? What if he—

The Prince of Darkness steps out from the forest.

And he's naked.

Like... butt naked.

His body dripping with water.

His muscles glistening in the light.

He walks toward me, his powerful legs carrying him easily, his abs twisting with each movement, pulling my eyes lower... lower... lower...

Is that a puppy?

Elias holds a black wolf cub in his hands, so small it fits in his palm.

I rub my chin, trying to keep my eyes on the cute fur-ball and nowhere else. "So... I'm a bit confused as to what series of events led to this," I say, gesturing at his impressive form.

"I needed a bath," he says simply, standing by the fire.

He's um... well, he's close. I have to turn away to um... you know, avoid seeing the fun bits, as it were.

"And the wolf cub?" I ask, clearing my throat. "Did you find a pet store in the forest?"

"He needed help," says Elias. He steps closer. "I forget how much humans have trouble with nudity. In Inferna, we have no such issues."

"Cleary," I say, breathing quickly. I mean, it's hot right? That fire's really effective.

"I'll see if the boat has extra clothes," says the prince.

"Right. Because yours magically vanished apparently."

"They were destroyed." He steps past me, and for the first time I see his back. Claw marks rip across his body, revealing flesh and bone and bits of skin hanging loosely.

"Holy shit," I yell. "What happened?"

"I faced a creature in the forest. It sought to kill the pup."

"So," I clasp my hands together. "You left to save a baby wolf?"

He raises an eyebrow, searching through the bags on the boat. "Why did you think I left?"

"Definitely not that reason," I say. "We need to bandage your back."

"I'll be fine," he says. "I'm already healing."

He is, but slowly. The wounds would kill a human. Probably most vampires. I'm not sure how he's still walking. "No way," I say, standing, hands on my hips. "I need you in top condition in case the White Rider shows up again, so cut the tough guy bullshit and bring me some bandages."

He pulls some out from a pack and turns back and—

Oh god.

I did not mean to see that.

I mean...

I totally would have looked away if I could, okay? I totally would have looked away.

Elias grins.

Cocky bastard.

Oh god. I did not mean to say cocky right now. Okay? I did not mean to use that specific word as I gaze at his impressive... um... body part... and try to... um...

What was I saying again?

Elias chuckles, pulling a fur blanket from the boat and wrapping it around his waist. Bastard had it ready.

He walks over to my side and sits on a rock by the fire, holding bandages in one hand, a puppy in the other.

I pull a green vial from my cloak, half expecting it to be turned into clay, but nope, still the same healing ointment, and begin applying it to the prince's back. "Does it hurt?" I ask.

"No," he says, his voice cold, his body still except for his shallow breaths.

"Liar," I say, but my voice lacks conviction. Seeing his back is causing *me* pain. I can only imagine what he's feeling.

Theo approaches cautiously, sniffing at the new wolf cub. The puppy whines, his tail wagging wildly as they study each other.

"What's his name?" I ask, running my hand over a patch of smooth skin. My fingers grow hot at the touch, and I pull away for a second, grabbing more ointment.

Elias stares into the fire, his mind in some far-off place. "Duke," he says finally, placing the pup down. Duke runs over to Theo, sniffing the kitten all over.

The little manticore looks skeptical at first, then pats Duke on the head, and they start playing, twisting in the dirt, pawing and nibbling at each other's fur.

I smile at their antics. "The little guy seems important to you."

"My father had a wolf," Elias says, as if that explains everything.

Though perhaps it does. "I heard about that," I say, recalling a story Uncle Sly likes to share. "Baron, right?"

Elias nods. "That's his son."

"Huh." I glance at the puppy biting at Theo's ear. "You really have to explain more, you know."

He says nothing.

I apply ointment to a particularly raw area, like an I-can-see-his-ribs situation. He doesn't flinch even once. Doesn't make a sound. This man has seen pain before. Pain I can't begin to imagine. And I've died like, at least fifty times in a variety of horrifying ways, so that's saying something, little bird. That's saying a lot of somethings.

"You said your crimes were exaggerated," I begin softly. "But how can someone exaggerate murder?"

"I've killed in self-defense," he says, his hands curling into fists. "Destroyed those who sought to destroy me first."

"Like?"

"Like assassins sent to kill the second child of the High King and Queen of Inferna."

Makes sense, but... I clench my jaw. "What of the massacre?"

He scoffs, a guttural sound with no joy. "I was framed."

I sigh, wishing he had said something else. Anything else, really. "Not to sound rude, but I've heard that one before."

"I wasn't there," he growls, his muscles tensing beneath my hands.

"But they say you killed a keeper and a dozen watchers."

"I wasn't there," he repeats, smashing his fist against the stone. "Perhaps someone used illusion."

I rub the ointment deep into his wounds. "But the survivors were three highly trained watchers. They would have seen through the spell."

He shrugs. "Perhaps they lied. Like Thalius is lying about you."

I freeze, almost dropping the vial. The council is not what I thought. The Order I was so proud to be a part of is full of treachery and deceit. A part of me still can't accept the truth. The truth that all my training, all my hard work, was in service to a group with malicious intent.

"They are not all corrupt," says Elias, as if he can see within my heart. "Some of them are good. The criminals you chased were real. Even me."

I clutch his back. "But you said—"

"I was framed for the massacre," he says. "But I have stolen, cheated and killed. I have lied and manipulated for my own gain. I have abandoned those who needed me most."

He pulls away from my touch and passes me the bandages. They are overdue, I realize. I rubbed the ointment much longer than needed, lost in his words, lost in the very closeness between us.

I bite my lip, working to dress his wounds. "If you're so terrible, then why try to stop the White Rider?"

"Because he's after me," says Elias.

"So kill or be killed, is that it?" I spit. "Do you care nothing for the innocents who will suffer if an eternal darkness falls?"

"They care nothing for me," he says somberly. He gazes into the flames, his hair drifting in the wind. When he speaks again, his voice is smoky and rough. "I was born second in line to the throne. My entire childhood, everything was about my older sister. What Aya needed. What Aya deserved. It wasn't her fault, of course. But I saw the way people flocked to her, flocked to see the true heir of Inferna and Avakiri, the future ruler of vampire and Fae. No matter what I did, I was never as good as her in their eyes."

He pauses, his nails digging into the stone, breaking the rock itself. "I acted out. As a child, I didn't know better. So I stole and lied and yelled for attention. The bad prince they called me around the castle. The little miscreant. Soon enough, word spread, and the common people spoke of deeds I had yet to do. He kills animals, they would whisper. He burned my house, they would say. They believed in my malice with such passion, I suppose I began to believe in it as well."

He turns his head to the side, and I catch a glimpse of his blue eyes. "When Father and Mother gave me my own castle, my own lands to oversee, I could not believe it. 'But the people hate me,' I said. 'They think I'm a criminal.' 'Then prove them wrong,' said my father. And I wanted to. I wanted to…"

"But you couldn't," I say quietly.

He shakes his head. "I tried at first, but rumors of my misdeeds continued to grow, and out of fear of failure, out of fear of disappointing my mother and father, I ran. I left Crimson Castle and my responsibilities. I left never to return."

Some things are always out of reach.

Like a place for me on the council. Sometimes, no matter how hard we try to move in one direction, the world tugs us in another.

I finish wrapping the last bandage and place my hands on his back, feeling the warmth of his flesh. But…

He's a vampire.

He shouldn't be so warm.

So hot.

He's burning up.

"Elias, how do you feel?"

He mumbles something under his breath.

"Elias—"

He falls forward, collapsing into the dust, his body convulsing. He's infected. The beast that attacked him poisoned his blood.

I pull out my blue vial, the mixture of antidotes, and pour the liquid down his throat. He spits most of it out, his neck tight, veins bulging as he tries to breathe. Duke runs to his side, whining and licking at his hair. Theo puts his paws on the prince's chest.

He's dying.

The potion isn't working.

But there must be a way.

"Feed on me," I say, falling to his side, holding my wrist to his mouth.

"No," he mumbles. "Not like this…"

"Feed on me!" I yell.

"No…"

I draw my dagger and cut a crimson line across my wrist, spilling red onto the snow beneath me. I push my hand over his mouth, letting blood flow down his throat.

He tries to turn away at first, but he's too weak, and his neck begins to convulse as he swallows the scarlet liquid. His eyes turn dark, and his teeth grip onto my wrist, tearing into my flesh, draining more of my blood.

He grabs my hand with his own. His strength is returning.

Theo growls cautiously. Duke whimpers.

I'm losing too much blood. Right.

I pull away, and Elias rolls to the side, licking up the last of the blood around his lips. His breaths are heavy and quick. His eyes are wild.

And then something else happens.

His form begins to diminish. His muscles begin to fade. As if he had fallen into a coma, unable to exercise for months. His skin turns a warmer shade. His eyes turn a duller blue. The power of his very presence wanes.

"What's happening?" asks Elias, looking at his hands. They are, to put it simply, normal. Just normal. I mean, he still looks like a movie star and model were superimposed into awesome. But, slightly less godly, perhaps.

"I think..." I say, my throat catching. "I think you're turning human."

CURE

*W*hat the F is this? And I'm not talking about Elias turning human. Or at least, less vampirey. I'm talking about this nasty ass booger that flew out of my nose. Shit looks green. Like an alien has taken residence in my brain. And yeah, I'm totally avoiding the bigger issue here. Because it's easier to pretend my blood didn't just cure vampirism. Because there is no cure for vampirism. Because I must be hallucinating, right? Or dreaming. Please let this be a dream.

Elias whispers some words I can't hear, and a pebble levitates over his hand. "I still have my magic," he says, his brows pinched. "I'm still Fae. But..." He clutches the giant boulder he recently cracked with his bare hands, palming its rough surface. "My strength is gone," he says softly, falling back.

Okay, wakey wakey now, Iris. Come on.

I close my eyes and count to three. On three, I will be awake, little bird. Mark my words.

One—

Two—

Three—

Shit, still here.

Okay, maybe I was wrong. Maybe he's not cured. Maybe he's just weak from recovering.

The wind picks up, and he wraps his arms around his body, shivering, and for the first time I see Elias Vane Spero feel cold. Ah crap.

He locks eyes with me. "My…"

Don't say it.

"Vampirism…"

Don't you dare say it.

"Is…"

Shut up.

"Gone."

Argh. What the F is this? I ask again, since nobody bothered to answer the first time.

My parents are supposed to be nobodies.

My blood is supposed to be poor.

Worse than poor.

Piss shit bad.

Not the cure to vampirism.

Maybe you're wondering why this is so bad, little bird. Well, let's see… if news of this got out, every vampire seeking to break their curse would want a piece of me. Literally.

The scholars would want to study me. And by study, I mean cut me open and categorize my insides in jars.

The businessmen and women would want to monetize me. Duplicate my blood if they can.

The witches, werewolves, and heck, anyone who has any kind of beef with the vampires—and let's be honest, that's a long ass list—would want to weaponize this power.

None of those options sound particularly appealing, so…

"Please don't tell anyone," I say.

Elias studies his hand as if seeing it for the first time. "Did you know?" His voice is harsh, tinged with disappointment.

"No," I say quickly. "If I knew, I'd never have offered my blood. Well, except you'd be dead. But, damn, I didn't mean to… change you."

He blinks, as if waking from a trance. Suddenly, he grabs the bandages and rushes to my side, clutching my wrist. Oh right. I'm bleeding. How easy it is to forget things sometimes.

Elias cleans my cut, pouring some alcohol over it from his flask, then applies ointment and dresses my wound. I totally do not squirm and curse and yell throughout the process. Nope. I'm cool as a cucumber. Which reminds me. Where did that saying come from? I mean, are cucumbers really that cool?

I ask Elias, because I need something to fill the silence between us.

He nods. "The inside of a cucumber is around twenty degrees cooler than its outside environment, even in hot weather."

Huh.

"But really," continues Elias. "To learn the origin of the term, you should ask my father. He would have been around at the time."

"Right. So…"

None of us bring up my blood. The cure. What I did to Elias. I think both of us want to pretend the last few minutes never happened, at least for a little while. But they did happen, didn't they? There's no going back.

"I'm sorry," I say softly. "For changing you."

He doesn't look at me, his eyes fixed on the bandages he wraps around my wrist. "It may not be permanent."

Wait. That's right. We don't know the full effects of this yet. His powers may return. Of course, things could also get worse. He could fall over and die spontaneously. Which is totally not reassuring.

Elias finishes dressing the wound, but he doesn't let go of my hand, clutching it tightly. "Don't be sorry, Iris. You saved me, remember. Without your blood, I'd be dead."

I want to say something kind in return. Instead I sneeze. All over him. Like my snot flies into his face. Like snotpocalypse has arrived. What is this? Am I allergic to the new Elias?

"Excuse me," I say, pinching my nose to avoid another incident.

"This…" he groans, wiping the nasty off his face with a cloth. "I can never forgive." He walks back to the boat and finally pulls out some actual clothes. While I keep sneezing, he dresses in brown leather garments and throws a black fur cloak over his shoulders. The clothes look a smidgen too big for him, like they would have fit him perfectly before… well… you know.

"You sound cute when you sneeze," he says playfully, and I'm glad some cheer has returned to him. "Like a mouse."

"Um… thanks?" I say, rubbing my poor leaky nose.

He chuckles and tosses a bow and quicker over his back. "I'll return with food."

Oh right. Like I thought he was going to do. But hey, I'll take a puppy any day.

Duke hops around, in good spirits now that Elias is healed. He tries to follow the prince into the woods.

"No," says Elias. "Stay."

The wolf cub sits.

"Good boy." The prince resumes his stride.

Duke follows.

"I said stay."

Duke nudges the prince's pants with his nose. Then starts biting at his boots.

Elias looks up to the heavens, sighing. "This is going to be difficult."

"Theo will keep an eye on him," I say. "Won't you, Theo?"

The manticore shifts to be slightly larger, twice the size of most cats, and runs over to the wolf cub, clutching the pup in his mouth like a mother would do. He brings Duke over by the fire, sitting down next to me. The pup tries to get back to Elias as soon as he's free, but Theo doesn't let him. What a good kitty.

"Thank you, Theo," says the prince.

He steps forward, moving slower than he did before he drank my blood, stumbling over a rock, as if he's uncomfortable with his very body. He sighs, pausing at the edge of the woods and glancing back at me. "You told me one of your parents was human, the other was not. Who was the other, Iris?" His gaze is penetrating. He wants answers. Wants them with all his being.

"My mother was human. My father…" my throat constricts.

"Yes?"

"He was…"

"Go on."

Just let it out, Iris. Just get it over with. "He was a bunyip, okay?"

Elias squints. "A bun what?"

Don't make me explain it. Please don't.

He says nothing.

Oh god, okay… "It's um… a monster that lives in swamps. Looks kind of like a cross between a dog and a worm." I plant my head in my hands, hiding my blushing cheeks. I so can't believe I'm actually sharing this with him.

"Oh, I know what a bunyip is," says Elias. "But I'm confused about how the mating would have occurred."

"Well it did, okay. It happened." I grab Theo and Duke, holding them close, letting their cuteness distract me from my misery.

"And you believe this because…"

I blink. "Because Sly told me."

Elias sucks in air quickly. "I'm sorry, Iris, but I think he lied to you."

"He…" He totally would have lied, wouldn't he? "But why? And why pick a bunyip?"

Elias shrugs. "To embarrass you? To discourage you from looking into your heritage?"

I sneeze, disturbing the cute fur balls on my lap. "That weasel." My hand curls into a fist. If my uncle were here… oh, he would feel the pain. Of my words, that is. Yes. He would feel some very painful words.

Elias leans back against a tree. "What else do you know of your parents?"

I take a deep breath. "Not much. Sly said he looked for them, but all he found was bits of information. They were homeless. They were staying at an abandoned house. They had me there. They couldn't raise me. So…" My throat grows tight. "So, they gave me up. They left me in front of the Black Lotus."

"I'm sorry," says Elias.

I shrug, gazing into the fire. "They never cared for me. So why should I care for them, right? They're nobodies who left their own kid. Selfish bastards." My breath hitches. My eyes water. It's just allergies, I tell myself. Nothing more. Certainly not a lifetime of pent-up abandonment issues. Definitely not that.

"Perhaps they didn't care for you," Elias says gently. "Or perhaps they *couldn't* care for you."

"Then they shouldn't have had a baby," I spit.

He nods. "They might have been selfish bastards. But clearly, they weren't nobodies." He raises his hand, devoid of its vampiric strength, as if to remind me of my blood, and then vanishes into the woods.

I drop my head, rubbing my temples, because I so feel a sinus headache coming on. Seriously, what's up, Inferna? Am I allergic to your plants or something?

I pull an orange vial from my cloak, a general pick-me-up concoction, and take a swig, hoping it will help. Now, how about I toss more logs on the fire, because it's getting chilly out here. Like extra chilly. Like…

Oh no.

Frost creeps over the water, turning the river into ice. The flames burn silver.

He'll come in the night
In armor of white
Riding a steed of snow

THE SONG IS FAINT. Distant. Coming from the woods. Elias!

Three signs there are
That mean he's not far
Silver army in tow

136

I RUSH INTO THE FOREST, drawing my daggers. Theo carrying Duke at my heels. Why is this happening now? Of all the possible times. It's like…

It's like he can sense when the prince is vulnerable.

Seriously.

First time, the rider shows up while Elias and I are trapped under rocks. Second time, he shows up after Sly has been poisoned. And now, third time, he shows up after Elias lost his strength and while I'm having an allergy attack. It can't be a coincidence. He knows we're weak. And he means to take advantage.

"Could have used the heads up, Silence," I say.

It takes a moment for the voice to respond. *I have many eyes and ears, but here I have only yours.*

"Right, whatever that means."

I cannot help you. You must protect Elias on your own. You must keep his blood safe from the rider.

Oh, I intend to, creepy voice. I intend to.

First comes the frost
Second the flame
Third are the voices
of those he has slain

I REACH a clearing in the forest, the song echoing louder than ever. A frozen pond spreads out before me. The White Rider stands on the ice, holding a struggling Elias in the air. The prince is no match without his vampiric strength.

"What have you done?" roars the rider, sniffing at his prey. "What have you done to his blood?"

I see. "Did we ruin your plans, rider?" I ask, twirling my daggers, Theo growing to full size behind me.

The creature looks my way, his silver eyes curious. "There is no cure. It's impossible. Unless…" He drops Elias, turning all of his attention to me. "Can it be?" he whispers.

Good. His focus is off Elias. Now I just need to—

The rider rushes forward, Moonlight Sword in hand, faster than I have ever seen.

And cuts my body in two.

RENEWAL

I return on a hill overlooking the frozen pond. Thank the gods renewal was up and running, because I did not see that shit coming. The rider rends his sword free of my old corpse and spins around, searching, searching as if…

Does he know I can come back?

Usually people assume I'm dead once they, well, kill me. But the rider must have figured it out. Or at least he suspects the truth.

Elias climbs onto his knees, his eyes fixed on my old body. "No," he shouts, grabbing his sword off the ice. "No!"

See? He thinks I'm dead.

And how sweet, he wants to avenge me.

Theo knows better, however. He stays low, waiting for my orders, holding Duke safely with his mouth.

"You will pay!" roars the prince, aiming his blade at the rider. Suddenly, his body convulses. His muscles grow.

He's…

He's turning back into a vampire.

Because I died.

The creature's eyes keep searching until he finds me.

I do a little wave.

He chuckles, turning to Elias. "Oh, if you only knew what she truly was, old friend."

Does he mean... Does he know what I am?

"I'm not your friend," yells Elias. "I have no clue who you are."

"You have tried to forget me," says the rider. "Tried to bury me. Along with the rest of your family's secrets. But I will not be forgotten." He swings the Moonlight Sword through the air, leaving a trail of light in its wake.

Okay, enough talking, time to run. And, oh look, my new body isn't sneezing anymore. So yay. Death = instant allergy cure. Whodathunkit?

I whistle and Theo lunges into the air, diving over the rider and landing by Elias. The prince glances at my body, his feet fixed in place.

The idiot.

"I'm alive!" I holler down the hill.

His eyes follow my voice. His gaze meets mine.

The rider charges.

Shit.

I throw one of my daggers.

It won't stop the creature.

He evades it with ease, spinning out of the way.

But it slows him down.

Just long enough for Elias to jump on top of the manticore.

They take to the air, swooping past me. I grab onto Theo's mane, pulling myself up alongside Elias.

The rider follows, his steed appearing beneath him.

"How are you still alive?" asks the prince, clutching onto my waist as we fly through the blizzard.

"Long story," I say through chattering teeth. I reach forward, pulling the wolf pup out of Theo's mouth and clutching him close to my chest.

"Tell me." The prince's tone is hurried, urgent.

"Well, I was blessed by the Mother Dryad." Okay, maybe it wasn't *that* long of a story after all.

"Do you actually remember this happening? Or did Sly tell you?"

I freeze. "Sly told me."

Focus, hisses Silence. *You must escape the rider.*

"Ah, pretty sure we're flying and he's not, so…"

But how long can you fly? How long before your beast grows tired?

"A couple of hours—"

The rider is tireless. You must find a way to slow him down.

"Great…" I glance down. Sure enough, the White Rider races through the forest, keeping pace below. We cross a lake. Yes, that should get in his way—

The water freezes below his steed's hooves, forming a path of ice.

Oh right.

The pup whimpers in my hands. The cold is getting to him. More of this blizzard and he might not make it.

"We need to find shelter," I yell over the wind. "Somewhere even the White Rider fears to tread."

Elias curses under his breath. "The Crimson Castle."

"Your old home? The place with the Twilight Bow?"

He nods. "There's a reason the bow is there. The castle is cursed."

"And you didn't mention this earlier because?"

"Would it have stopped you?"

"No." I need that bow. I need to stop the rider. "But a heads-up would have been nice."

"I told you I didn't want to go back." He points forward. "Take a left at that river, Theo. It will lead us to the castle."

The manticore speeds up, gliding along the water.

I pull my cloak tighter around the freezing pup. "Hey Silence, do you think this plan will work?"

It may. The voice is softer than usual. *After Elias abandoned the castle, a vampire called Malcar took over the realm. He dug deep into the earth, searching for treasures. Instead he found a darkness.*

"Okay… but if this darkness is too much for the rider, how are we going to stand a chance?"

You are more powerful than you know, Iris.

"Care to elaborate?"

Not now. Not this way. We don't know who else may be listening.

Who else... "You mean, there might be other people in my head?"

Yes. We must be careful.

What the hell? Since when did my brain become the local Wi-Fi hotspot?

We fly over a hill of evergreen trees, emerging into a valley of snow torn in two by a sparkling river. In the distance, a jagged mountain covered in white looms over the land, and at its peak stands a pale-blue fortress.

Crimson Castle.

Gargoyles perch on its frost-tipped ledges, dark stained windows, and mismatched towers. Twisted spires erupt from its arched ceilings. The citadel is a monstrosity, and yet I can't look away. There is a cruel beauty to the structure. A genius to its mad design.

But why is it called crimson when the walls are blue, almost silver, like.... Oh, I see...

Streams of red liquid flow down from the mountain, like crimson tears pelting the snow. "Is that... blood?" I ask, squinting through the blizzard.

"No," yells Elias over the wind. "It's clay leaking from the earth. There are endless deposits beneath the stronghold."

A natural phenomenon then. Still... when the wind blows, it's as if I can hear the castle speak. Even breathe. I glance at the fortress again, and for a moment I see it as a woman draped in silver, trapped alone on a mountain of frost, weeping blood for all she has lost.

Just my wacky imagination, of course. Nothing more.

I look down at the rider. Bastard is still on our tail. I pat Theo on the head. "Initiate plan: Escape White Rider by entering cursed castle." I mean, what can go wrong with that, right?

Theo dives down toward the open gate, piercing the blizzard like an arrow. The chill cuts at my skin, covering my hair and eyelashes in frost. My teeth chatter uncontrollably. My hands tremble.

We swoop past the threshold, the rider on our heels, and crash land onto the stone floor, sliding through a dark hall. Theo digs his claws into the bricks, slowing us down, turning us back toward the entrance. My poor manticore is breathing heavily, consumed with exhaustion. There will be no more flying. No more running. This better work.

The White Rider storms toward the gateway, unfazed by the castle. Crap. Well then—

His steed rears backwards on all fours, whining and backing away. The rider's eyes grow wide, staring at something.

Something in the shadows. Something within the fortress. Something I cannot see.

He yanks on his reins hard, turning his horse away and rushing back into the blizzard, disappearing into the night.

"Bloody hell," gasps Elias. "I can't believe it worked."

My eyes stay fixed on the corner of the hall, on the shadows gathering there. What did the rider see within?

"We need to go deeper," roars Elias, grabbing the wolf from my hands and pulling me from my thoughts. "We need to find warmth."

I nod, following him into the belly of this twisted abomination. This place he once called home.

Theo shifts to kitten size and jumps on my shoulder, resting against my neck as we reach the end of the hall, stopping at a pair of stairs. They lead to an empty throne carved from gray stone, illuminated by a single beam of moonlight from a window. There are no tapestries here. No banners. No torches. The place is gloomy. Sad. In need of a decorator. I can see why Elias left.

"This way," says the prince, his voice ragged and tired. He leads me to the side, up a winding stairway to the second floor, and into a room at the end of the hallway. It is dark, and I follow him mostly by sound rather than sight. He closes the door behind us and rushes to a corner, picking something up off the ground. Rocks. Flint. He hits the stone against his sword, casting sparks, starting a flame near the wall. A fireplace, I realize, my eyes adjusting to the new light. He's lighting the fireplace.

I sit down on a fur rug in the glow of the warmth, holding poor Theo in my lap while Elias holds Duke. He sets the pup down beside me, and runs over to a bed that fills a large corner of the spacious room, pulling off blankets and sheets and tossing them over me and the animals, leaving none for himself.

"You'll freeze," I say.

He stands by the fire, sluggishly rubbing his hands together, his fur cloak dripping with melting snow. "I'll b-b-be fine," he says through chattering teeth. "My vampirism is returning."

"Clearly not fast enough." I open up the blankets, gesturing him to come closer. I can't believe I'm saying this but... "We need to share body heat."

"I'll b-b-b—"

He falls forward, barely catching himself against the wall, then slips down to the floor. He's passing out, the idiot. I pull him close against my body, wrapping the blankets around us both. His touch is cold, but his breath is warm, misting in the air as it curls around my skin. He tries to mumble something, but I put my fingers against his trembling lips, silencing him. My fingers linger longer than they should, and when I finally pull away, I lean down, resting my head against his chest.

I can hear his heartbeat. Like thunderous hooves storming through a field. I can smell his scent. Like a forest of fresh leaves and pine. The prince's body is rock solid, a slab of muscle and bone. His face is the most handsome I have ever seen. His skin a warm burnt-orange against the flames. His eyes a piercing blue.

I just want to rub my hands all over—

Snap out of it, Iris. It's just that paranormal mojo making you hot and heavy again. Unless... it's not? His unnatural pull has been fading. And his vampirism hasn't fully returned.

But then what's up with all the out of control hormones?

Don't be an idiot, Iris. He's a criminal, remember?

Right. But...

Man, I wish I had my best friend to talk to right now. No offense, little bird. But Callie is, you know, Callie, so...

Think, Iris. Think. What would Callie do in a situation like this?

Well, she'd probably start removing all his clothes for some extra 'body heat', and then—

Nope. Never mind. Bad idea.

And oh look, Elias is asleep, so no point worrying about this anyway. Finally, he gets to feel the fatigue we non-vampires experience every day. Theo and Duke are passed out too. So that leaves me. Well, me and...

"Silence?" I whisper.

The voice doesn't respond.

"Silence?"

Nothing.

"What, you go to sleep too?"

I guess it's possible. I'm not even sure what Silence is. Or if I can trust it. But Callie put us together. That must mean something.

The succubus has been my best friend for nearly my entire life. For many years, she was the only other child around at the Black Lotus. Something about her mother always being a guest, until her mother died that is, and her mother died pretty young. So Sly took Callie under his wing, just as he did me, and the two of us did everything together.

We'd play hide and seek in the halls. Sneak through the secret passages. Pretend we were undercover agents and that some of the guests were evil villains who needed spying on. We'd mark and track our targets. Collect intel. And then, one day, we turned our games into careers. I became a hunter. Callie became an ambassador. A sort of peace envoy between different races at the hotel. She helped smooth over grudges. Settle debts. Prevent mass destruction, that sort of thing.

I wonder if she's found safety. Or if Thalius got to her. If she's rotting in a cell next to Sly. I just have to find this bow and get the Moonlight Sword back. I need to prove their innocence.

These are my mental musings as we sit in front of the fire, the heat slowly pulling the numbness from our bodies, my stomach growling in despair, yelling "Feed me, Iris. Feed me!" When none of us are shaking anymore, and the kitten and pup are cuddled together, resting against Elias, I creep around the room, scouring for snacks. Oh look, a silver platter, and inside...

Yuck, it looks like a turd made of ash. I'm pretty sure this was edible like one hundred years ago. So, no thank you, chef. Hard pass on that one.

What do we have here? Another platter. Perhaps this one will have—

"Ahh!" I yell, literally jumping backwards into the air.

Elias catches me in his arms as I fall down. "What happened?" he asks, his eyes scanning the room.

I scream again, pointing to the plate. "There are only three things I'm afraid of. And one of them is right there."

CRIMSON CASTLE

*E*lias follows my gaze.

"There's nothing there," he says, squinting at the silver platter, putting me down on my feet.

"What?" I yell, totally not hiding behind his big, manly, broad shoulders. "How can you not see it?" Because it's there. Huge. Monstrous. Looking at me with a thousand eyes. Threatening to eat my insides. It's... It's... I can barely speak its name. It's... "It's a giant hairy ass spider!"

"A spider?" asks Elias. "You're scared of a spider?"

He chuckles. And not just a little chuckle. No. This is a grip your belly and laugh like Santa kind of chuckle. This is a *not* taking the situation seriously at ALL kind of chuckle! If I were to describe this chuckle in a text, I would simply write: ROFLMAO. Because that's what kind of chuckle this bastard is performing!

How dare he!

I feel like punching something.

And then eating it.

>:(

"Get rid of it!" I command. "Theo. Attack."

My kitten glances at the giant spider bigger than my entire hand, yawns, and goes back to sleep. WTF? This can't be.

"Where is this little spider anyway?" asks Elias between his bouts of laughter.

"Uh… like right over there." I point at the deadly creature. The beast that consumes my nightmares.

"Where?"

"The platter."

The prince steps forward. "There's nothing on the—Oh bloody hell!" He jumps back, grabbing his bow and aiming an arrow at the eight-legged arachnid.

I sigh in relief. "Finally!"

"That's no spider," he hisses. "That's a hell viper!"

"A hell what now?"

"A hell viper," he repeats, circling the giant spider. "Its venomous bite will kill you in a matter of seconds."

I nod. "Now that I can believe. But why—"

"Be careful. Its tail will grow spikes at the first sign of aggression."

I raise an eyebrow. "Its tail? Pretty sure spiders don't have tails."

"I told you. It's no spider, it's a—"

"A hell viper, right." I cross my arms. "I don't think you're seeing what I'm seeing."

He keeps his eye on the spider/viper. "What do you mean?"

"I mean… it's an illusion." I toss my dagger at the spider and—poof—the arachnid bursts into black smoke, fading away as my blade lodges itself into the silver platter.

Elias lowers his bow, the muscles in his face relaxing. "The curse…"

I nod, rending my dagger free. "A nightmare curse, at least level three. It knows our fears, then makes them visible."

The vampire walks up cautiously to the plate, studying it from all angles. "You know your curses."

"Guess what the number two paranormal crime is."

"Interesting… Out of curiosity, if curses are number two, what's number one?"

"Illegal feeding off humans, of course."

He nods, looking uneasy at my answer.

But what can I say? "Vampires have trouble controlling their urges."

He scoffs. "A little stereotypical, aren't we?"

"What's that supposed to mean?"

"It means not all vampires are blood-sucking monsters." He turns on me, closing the distance between us, towering over my much smaller body. "I can assure you, I have no trouble resisting my urges, Iris. When I drink from a woman, it's because she wants me to." He brushes back my hair with his hand, gazing at me with his gorgeous eyes, and I understand what he means. There are many women who would do anything for a man like this. Be anything he wanted. Look any way he pleased.

But not me.

I turn away, breaking eye contact and looking at the fire.

Elias sighs, his tone softer than before. "You're lucky, Iris. Even being half-human, no one assumes you're a monster by default. That you're a criminal just waiting to be caught."

His words, so light and delicate, hit me like a hammer in my chest. Vampires have a bad rep, it's true, but so do mutts like me. People judge us by our race before we even utter a single word. And here I am, doing the same. "I'm sorry," I say gently. "I'll be more careful with my words in the future."

Elias grins. "Remember, Iris, there is beauty in all things. Even in a banished prince like me. Even in an outcast half-breed like you." He steps closer, pausing. "Especially in an outcast half-breed like you."

Okay, is it just me, or is it getting too hot in here? Maybe time to put out the fire. Crack open a window. Maybe... um... what was I thinking again? Oh yeah, the curse....

I turn away from Elias, and oh wow, it's a little cooler already as I walk over to the window. I try to open the latch, but the damn thing is stuck and—

Elias slides his hand over mine. "Here, like this." He guides my motions, pulling up on the latch and then to the side, opening a window that has likely stayed closed for a century.

The wind is cold and fresh against my face, but my fingers still burn under the prince's grasp. Right, um... I clear my throat, moving away, because I really need to focus, and Elias is not conducive to such things.

I sit down on a chair, kicking my legs up on the nearby table, placing my hand under my chin. I call this the 'casual thinker' pose. Perfect for such occasions. "I need more intel. Where is the Twilight Bow located exactly?"

"No idea. I never saw the artifact while I ruled," says Elias, walking back to the fire. "My guess is, whoever placed it here, did so after I left, and after the curse."

"Because they thought this was the perfect hiding place," I continue. "No. Hiding place is the wrong word."

"What do you mean?" asks Elias.

"The bow is less hidden. More protected. After all, it's in a giant abandoned castle. Not the most discreet location, exactly. The Moonlight Sword was in the Black Lotus dungeon hanging in a beam of light. Also, not the most discreet location. Think about it. It's as if someone isn't trying to hide the artifacts but rather—"

"Lock them behind a challenge," finishes Elias, his eyes growing wider.

"Like the puzzle you solved to get the sword," I say, snapping my fingers. "Someone wanted to keep the artifacts out of the wrong hands, but they also wanted them accessible in the future. In case—"

"In case the First Vampire was ever awoken," says Elias, finishing my sentence again. Is this becoming a thing between us? I think it's becoming a thing, and I'm not sure how to feel about that.

I nod. "Right. So, this challenge must be the curse. We lift the curse and we get the bow. At least, that's the idea."

Elias shrugs. "It's worth a try."

I lean forward, resting my head in my hands. "Okay, so what do we know about the curse so far?"

"Each of us sees something different," says Elias. "Our own fears."

"And sometimes, we'll see things where others see nothing," I add. "That's what must have happened below. The White Rider witnessed something we didn't. That's why he ran."

"But why would the curse cause him to flee and not us?"

I shrug. "Well, there are different degrees of fear. Some people have phobias that can render them paralyzed. Others, like us, have more mild fears."

"Like spiders?" he asks, teasingly.

"Exactly." I pause. "Okay, time to solve this shit. But first..." I clutch my grumbling stomach. "Iris need food."

Elias chuckles, grabbing an old torch from the wall and lighting it in the fireplace. "Come on. I know where the emergency supplies are kept."

In a few minutes, we're downstairs in an abandoned kitchen enjoying a lovely meal of Inferna dried mushrooms. And by lovely, I mean I want to gag as I devour the turd-like substance, but hey, there's nothing else to eat. It all went rotten ages ago.

Duke and Theo also partake in the 'exquisite' cuisine, albeit with less complaining. The wolf pup looks larger than before. Like, unnaturally larger.

Elias notices me studying the wolf. "His father is no normal animal," says the prince. "I expect neither is he."

Curious. Vague. But curious.

"You know," I say through a mouthful of mushroom. "We may have to destroy the Unseen Lord at the end of this. I hope, when the time comes, you won't hesitate, considering he's your great grandfather and all."

Elias chuckles. "A common misconception, that. You see my father was turned by my grandmother. So, technically I share no blood relation to Lucian, the man most call my grandfather, or Lucian's brother, or their father, the so called Unseen Lord."

Huh. "Good to know." Something catches my eye. A symbol carved around a doorway. Dozens of times, like scratches in the stone. Three claw marks over a spiral.

I step closer, bidding Elias to bring the torch. "Were these here when you ruled?" I ask.

"No," he says, studying the wall. "The markings are in the ancient tongue. They say, *Be wary all who enter the spider's lair.*"

"You know ancient Fae?" I ask, trying not to sound too impressed, but, to be honest, I'm hella impressed.

"My Uncle Tavian taught me," says the prince, though he sounds sad when he says it. Clearly, there's a story there. But we don't have time to share.

"This isn't a curse," I say quickly. "It's a monster. A level nine nightmare."

He frowns. "How can you be sure?"

"Because I've seen these markings before." In another time. Another place. The memories crawl their way to the surface, but I shove them back down.

"And because it makes sense," I continue. "Nightmares feed off fear. They're drawn to places like this: abandoned houses, deserted villages, old castles. It makes their work easier."

"Are you sure?" asks Elias. "Because they say a vampire called Malcar dug deep into the earth for riches, and unleashed a terrible curse—"

"And everyone in the castle died, blah blah blah. Sometimes, fools still venture inside, seeking the unrecovered treasure, only to never return, blah blah blah. It's a lie. Probably started by the Nightmare herself. She needs to terrify people, right? So, she picks a castle with a dark history as her lair, but she still needs said people, so she starts a story about treasure, luring adventurers and fools alike. Classic textbook scenario."

He rubs his chin, shaking his head skeptically.

"Fine. Need another clue? If this were a curse, I'd be seeing spiders everywhere. But I'm not, because the monster isn't aware we're here yet. When I opened the platter upstairs, I set off a ward she placed. The White Rider set off another by trying to enter the castle on foot. When the monster finally finds us, I promise you, our fears will not cease unless we defeat the creature."

Finally, he nods slowly. "Okay... So how do we stop this nightmare?"

I walk forward and push open the large door, drawing my dagger (I really need a replacement for the one I threw at the rider) as I step through the passageway. "That's tricky. I've never defeated a level nine nightmare before. But in theory, stabbing them through the heart should work."

A dark hallway winds before us, the slope ascending to the higher parts of the castle.

"Stabbing?" asks Elias, following me. "Don't you usually bring your marks in alive?"

I clench my jaw. "Not this time."

The ancient symbols cover the entire ceiling and both walls, their number multiplying as we venture upwards.

As we reach the end of the hall, a cool breeze swirls around us and a pale golden light blinds me for a moment. Daylight, I realize. The sun has begun to rise. We step into a courtyard covered in snow, surrounded on all sides by white pillars and rosebushes that twist and turn like a maze. The flowers aren't dead, as one would expect. Instead, the roses are frozen, sparkling like diamonds. The wind here is fierce, and the clouds swirl closely above. We are high up, near the top of the castle. Near the heavens themselves.

Theo hisses at my side. Duke growls.

And I see what they have already heard.

A figure steps from behind the pillars, entering the courtyard. They are draped in a cloak dark as night, the withered fabric trailing behind them like a tail, their face covered in shadow. The nightmare is here.

My uncle once told me everything is connected. Everything has a purpose. I suppose you agree, don't you, little bird? That's why you're reading this, after all. To see how one event connects to the other. To understand how my battle with this creature leads to what I will become. Know this, I never set out to become the monster. The one you whisper of in the quiet of night.

But a monster I am.

And I regret nothing.

If you think things have been dark so far, then I recommend you stop reading now. Because I can assure you they only get darker.

A SHORT STORY

*M*aybe you think this is an adventure story. Maybe even a romance.

You're wrong.

It's a horror.

And it's time you knew the beginning. Because to understand what happens next, you must first understand me.

Why I fear spiders.

Why I became who I am.

Why I need to join the council.

I touched on this tale when the White Rider stabbed Callie in the chest. I said I had no time to go into details then.

I lied.

Because I am afraid. Of what happened before and what may yet happen again. Of the memories seared into my mind. Of legs crawling on my skin and a figure wrapped in shadow.

But now I must face the truth. Because the past has returned. The monster that got away is here.

And it's time I end her once and for all.

* * *

I STAND in a field of reeds, clutching the iron key in my hand, the sky a deep orange mixed with purple clouds. Finally, I am here. At the shack.

It groans before me, creaking in the wind, its wooden walls old and rotting. I step inside, necklace in one hand, dagger in the other. I am here to bring death to the murderer. To end the witch in the woods.

* * *

BUT I'M GETTING AHEAD of myself. We must go back further still. Back to when I was a little girl exploring a summer villa. Back to when I met *her*.

My tale begins in the Italian countryside, in a sprawling manor of golden stone, full of servants and butlers and strange guests coming and going, but entirely devoid of children except for myself. We were at the villa because of Sly. Because it was our 'summer vacation', as he called it, though he spent most of it working, so I'm not sure why he called it a vacation at all.

The adults were doing adult things in the study, chief among them, smoking pipes and reading long ponderous tomes, and as these things didn't appeal to me, I began to wander.

Like a brave journey-women, I took to the wilds, and in so doing found my entertainment. The countryside was full of bugs to find and categorize and name. Full of forests to explore and map. At first, my projects progressed slowly, for I worked alone, like a wandering bard on an epic quest. But as in most quests, it wasn't long until I met a companion.

Her name was Erullia. And she was a girl much like myself, around my height and age, by which I mean she was petite and barely ten. We were both pale and often dirty. Both prone to losing our shoes and playing games of riddles. We did, however, differ in our hair. Mine was straight and neat and black and short. Hers was long and unruly and the color of golden straw. I wanted hair like hers. She wanted hair like mine.

So it is often with children. They want what they see in others, because they have yet to look within. At least Erullia said something of the like, and I found it a deep and ponderous thought. We soon became an unstoppable team.

Rivers would not halt our progress, for we would find fallen logs to cross, or, if none were available, make rafts with our bare hands. Animals would not deter us, for Erullia had a way with them, as if she could speak their language. Sometimes, when it grew dark and cold and we felt monsters watching from the night, she would pull out her necklace from below her shirt and hold the black iron key before us like a shield. It was her good luck charm, she said, and it must have worked, for no harm befell us. At least, not at the time.

We always returned home before midnight. Me to the villa. Erullia to the nearby town. But as the summer stretched on and the days grew shorter, our expeditions became longer and more daring. It seemed as if we were searching for something yet to be found, for at the end of each day, Erullia would stoop her shoulders and lower her head and sigh and say 'tomorrow then.' One evening, as we set by a makeshift fire, I asked her what she meant.

And she told me of a witch in the woods.

"She lives in a shack in the forest, and all the insects of this land do her bidding," said Erullia. "They are her spies, and I suspect that is why we are yet to find her."

I remember shivering then, because I did not understand. Why would you want to find a witch?

"Because she took my brother, Mika," explained Erullia. "He loved exploring, following ant trails most of all. But one day he followed them too far, deep into the forest, and he never returned. The ants lured him into a trap, and the witch ensnared him. She wrapped him in a cocoon of silk and hung him in her shack. I must find him soon, or she will lay eggs in his body, and they will eat him alive as they hatch."

She grabbed my hands. "Please don't desert me, Iris. Please help me save my brother."

I swore I would aid her, and so that night I returned to the villa and interrupted one of the meetings in the study. I told Sly of the witch in the woods and the poor boy, Mika. The people he met with told me to leave. They said they were a council with important matters to discuss and no time for fairy tales. If there were a witch in the woods, they would know of her, for they were versed in such matters, or so they claimed. My uncle was not as harsh, but he too said he was busy, and that we would have to converse another time. But we were out of time. Didn't they understand? Mika would soon be eaten alive.

Someone suggested I be confined inside, for clearly my imagination ran too wild, and so before they finished I ran out of the villa. Erullia waited by the forest, as she always did, and together we set out on our final journey.

We traveled farther than we ever had before, and I remember my hands shaking as we crept over branches prone to snapping, hoping the insects would not catch sight of us and report our whereabouts to the witch. At some point, I suggested we cover ourselves in mud to better blend into the darkness, and after Erullia approved of the plan, we rolled around in the dirt near the banks of a river. The muck was cold and thick, and I could barely see my own friend behind the layers of grime after we were done.

"How will we stop the witch?" I asked.

Erullia pulled a dagger from her pack. "With this," she said, and I saw in her eyes she had used the blade before.

I needed a weapon of my own. So, I found a stick, and Erullia used her dagger to make it into a spear. She seemed skillful in woodwork, and she told me her mother died and her father had been a carpenter until a heavy piece of wood crushed his leg. That is why he could not search for Mika in the forest. That is why she had to do this alone.

"Not alone," I said, and we pressed on.

It wasn't long until we came upon the shack.

It stood amidst a field of reeds, groaning in the wind, its wood a pale blue in the moonlight. Shadows moved within, and I knew it was the witch and her insects.

My guts twisted in knots, and I stepped behind a bush to relieve my bowels. When I finished, I joined Erullia near the door, holding my spear at my side. I tried not to look at my friend, for I did not wish for her to see the fear on my face, when it seemed she had so little of her own.

"For Mika," said Erullia, and she stepped inside.

I followed her into the darkness. There was a rancid smell in the air, and I imagined it was the smell of death. There was a crunching noise below my boots, and I imagined it was a hundred insects dying below my heel. I could not see, and this scared me most of all, because how could someone fight what they could not see?

"Erullia," I whispered, reaching out with my hand, hoping to grab her collar. Instead, I grabbed something soft like butter. It oozed between my fingers, making a sucking noise, and I pulled away, biting down on my tongue to stop from screaming, because I did not wish for the witch to find me.

My mouth tasted like fire and iron, and I realized I must have drawn blood.

A light flickered in the distance, like a flashlight turning on and off, only there was no flashlight and only the light. It illuminated something white and fuzzy, though I could not make it out from where I stood. It did not seem to be the witch, however, and so I drew closer, holding my spear forward. I could make out bits of webbing holding something against the wall.

And as I came closer, I could see the thing.

Except it was no *thing* at all.

But a boy.

His skin pasty white and covered in worms.

A centipede sliding out from his mouth.

A spider crawling over his eye.

His rotten lips cracked open as he whispered, "Help me."

I bent over, retching though my stomach was empty.

"Iris!" yelled Erullia from behind me.

I turned and the moonlight filled the shack, illuminating all.

Dozens of cocoons hung from the ceilings, bits of fingers and toes sticking out from the webbing. Thousands of spiders swarmed the floor, crawling over my boots and my legs. And in the center of it all, stood a figure in a dark cloak, their face a black pit of shadow, their entire body hidden from view. The witch in the woods.

She stood behind Erullia, three times the size of my friend.

"Run!" I yelled, spitting blood onto the floor.

But Erullia did not move. Nor did she speak again.

And then I realized why.

A web spread over her body, and it had already tied her feet and gagged her mouth. One of her hands was still free however, and with it she tossed me her dagger. I caught the blade in the air.

The witch's cloak began to part down the center, and eight insect legs sprouted forward, wrapping themselves around Erullia and lifting her into the air. She looked so small, like a doll hanging on strings. The witch squeezed with her arachnid legs, and I heard a crunch, and Erullia went limp, her eyes staring blankly out the window. The cord around her neck snapped, and the iron key fell with a heavy thud.

She was dead, and I did not wish to die.

So, I screamed.

And I ran.

Somewhere along the way, I picked up the necklace, tears burning my eyes as I fled through the forest.

I reached the villa safely, and I woke Sly in the middle of the night, screaming and telling him of the witch and Erullia. He held me close and stroked my hair and told me he would help. The next day, we went into town to find Erullia's father, but he was nowhere to be found. The nearby folk said the carpenter had died years ago, and they'd never heard of a girl named Erullia, though children had gone missing of late. Sly asked me if I was playing a trick on him, because he did not like to be tricked.

I spat blood at his feet and stormed back into the woods, drawing the dagger I had hidden away in my pack. It was day this time around, and in the day the journey was much less frightful. This time, I will not run, I thought. This time, I will fight.

I stood in a field of reeds, clutching the iron key in my hand, the sky a deep orange mixed with purple clouds. Finally, I was here. At the shack.

It groaned before me, creaking in the wind, it's wooden walls old and rotting. I stepped inside, necklace in one hand, dagger in the other. I was here to bring death to the murderer. To end the witch in the woods.

But she was gone.

The shack was empty.

Sly appeared before me, his face red. He was not happy I ran, but he did help me search the shack. We found nothing but symbols scratched around the door. Three claw marks over a spiral that even Uncle Sly could not decipher. And as the sun began to set, I had to admit: the witch had moved on.

I fell on my knees and clutched the iron key and I swore I would catch the monster. I would become a hunter and avenge my friend.

And one day, I would sit on the council, and I would not assume I knew all there is to know, and that children are safe from witches. I would listen to children who speak of monsters. And I would keep them safe.

I placed the necklace around my neck. And I left the shack behind.

For years, I would not find the witch.

Until now.

* * *

I WAS A FOOL THEN. I didn't know what I know now.

The witch could have killed me in the shack, and yet she didn't. Why?

Because she needed my fear. Needed it to grow and fester so she could leach it from me.

And so, there was no carpenter.

No boy Mika.

No little girl.

There was only…

"Erullia. The witch in the woods."

The hood on the creature falls back, revealing the face of a beautiful woman, her lips stained black, purple mascara under her eyes. She giggles, sounding so much like my friend from years ago. "Took you long enough, Iris. Now tell me, where is my key?"

TWILIGHT BOW

"*T*he girl you knew as Erullia lived once," said the witch, pacing the courtyard. "I lured her to the forest and fed on her fear, until her mind became broken and her body weak. The girl you met, the form I took, was based on her. And it served me well. Many children I lured into the woods to save poor Mika. And in the end, they all died screaming. All but one. A girl with hair short and straight and black. A girl with darkness in her eyes. What are you, Iris? How did you break free of my spell? How did you steal my key?"

I grip the necklace around my neck until my knuckles turn white. "As to what I am, witch… I am your doom. As to how I broke free… I have a power you should never have trifled with. And as to your key… you can have it back."

I rush forward, ramming the iron into her throat, tearing through her jugular.

Black blood erupts from her mouth. Her eyes curl back into her head.

"You will never harm a child again," I hiss, driving the key deeper into her rotten flesh.

She chokes and mutters. And then she laughs. "Oh Iris. Did you think it would be so easy?"

She steps back, leaving the key in my grip. A hole remains in her throat, oozing thick black liquid, but she speaks as if uninjured, her lips curling in a smile. "It has been too long since I fed." She licks her lips, parting the front of her coat, and a shadow rushes forth, wrapping the world in darkness.

The courtyard is gone.

The wind has died.

I am alone.

In a pit of midnight with no sky.

I am back in the shack.

Unseen insects crawl over my boots.

Nails scratch in the distance.

Keep it together, Iris. This is only an illusion.

Elias is probably seeing his own nightmare. Theo and Duke as well. They will be no help here. I must escape this terror on my own.

I did so before.

I will do so again.

"I don't fear you," I yell. It's a lie, but I hope it sounds true.

Erullia chuckles, and her voice surrounds me. "What a fool you are, Iris. A little girl asks you to follow her into the woods, and you do so without hesitation. Your uncle tells you your parents are nothing, and you believe him without a second guess. How pitiful. No wonder the council will never promote you."

"Shut up," I hiss, slashing my dagger through the air and hitting nothing.

"Looking for me?" asks Erullia. Her voice so close. Right behind me.

I turn to face her.

But she is no longer the woman in the cloak.

Instead I am faced with my own reflection. Her skin a pale blue in the shadow. The witch studies her new body. "So, this is what you fear most of all. Is it because you left your uncle to rot in a cell? Or perhaps because you never went searching for your friend, Callie?" She steps forward. "Or maybe a part of you knew your uncle was lying to you all along. Maybe you wanted to hide the truth as much as he did. The truth of what you really are."

I strike forward with my dagger.

She does the same.

Our blades lock.

"I don't fear you," I repeat again.

"You can't lie to me, Iris," she whispers. "I know your heart. I know your soul."

"You know nothing," I roar, slicing at her legs.

She does the same to mine, and our blades meet again, ringing in the endless night.

"Do you want to see your true form?" she asks, smiling wide. "I can show you."

I strike again.

She blocks with my exact movement. "Witness the monster within." Her lips curl back in a snarl. Her veins turn black, bulging from beneath her skin. Her eyes burn red. When she screams, the entire world shakes at the sound.

That isn't me.

It can't be.

And yet...

Ever since I can remember, I have felt something within me. Something I can't explain.

"Fight me!" roars Erullia. "Slay me like the monster I am."

I raise my dagger, ready to strike, and yet, something gives me pause. For when I look upon my reflection, I see a beast, yes, but I also see a girl. A girl who tried so hard to never be afraid. A girl who sought to hunt monsters so she would never be the hunted again. And yet, in the end, she could never escape her fear. Because it was always within her.

I let the dagger slip from my fingers, and it falls to the ground with a clatter.

"What are you doing?" hisses the witch, her own blade sliding free from her grasp.

I fall to my knees, clutching the iron key around my neck. "I do fear you," I say softly. "I always have."

The black veins fade. The red eyes dim.

"Maybe I am a monster," I whisper. "But I regret nothing. So, strike me down, if you must. I'll fight myself no longer."

The witch falls to her knees before me. "Don't you understand, girl? My insects come for you. They will devour you whole."

The patter of a thousand legs grows around me. Spiders crawl up my pants. Centipedes weave up my arms. "Let them come," I say. "You want me to fight. You want me to run. And so, I'll do neither."

"You fool!" spits the witch. "I will break your mind. I will destroy your body."

"You can try."

She howls, her voice tearing the very air, and the darkness rips apart, drifting away like burned paper. The witch herself follows, breaking into three black crows and taking to the skies. The cold wraps around me, for I sit in the courtyard on a layer of frost. And where the witch once stood, now a silver bow hangs in the air. It glitters in the morning light, wisps of white smoke falling from its ashen frame.

I stand. And in my hand, I clutch the Twilight Bow.

It's light as a feather, and when I pluck its string, it seems to sing a soft melody. I toss the artifact over my shoulder and search my surroundings.

Theo and Duke shiver by a pillar, and when they see me, they run to my side. I pet them both and whisper soothing sounds in their ears, hoping to take their minds off the nightmares they just witnessed. They calm in time, following at my heel.

Elias is nowhere to be seen. He must have found a way to flee the illusion. Very well then. I walk back into the castle, searching for the lost prince. Though I walk through shadowed halls, the Twilight Bow shimmers across my back, lighting the way before me.

When I finally find the prince, it's in the bathhouses. He sits with his back against a pillar, shirtless once more, his tattoos rippling in the light of the torches he lit. His body is covered in cuts, as if a thousand claws sliced at his skin. He seems to have applied some sort of oint-ment to the wounds. A thick white salve. His breath is heavy, but when he sees me, he smiles. "You found the bow."

I nod. "What happened to you?"

"The creature attacked me," he says, gesturing to his wounds. "The top half of its body was that of a woman, the bottom half that of spider, and it tore at me with its claws. My sword did nothing to harm the nightmare, so I fled."

"Felt a sudden need for a bath?" I ask, grinning.

"I figured I would find salves and ointments here." He pulls some-thing from the shadows, lifting a bottle into the air. "But the wine was a pleasant surprise." He takes a sip, then passes me the drink.

I sit down across from him, putting the bow on the tile between us. "You left me alone. Not to mention Theo and Duke."

"I'm sorry." He pauses. "But I had no doubt you would defeat the beast. Though tell me, how did you finally manage the deed?"

"I starved her," I say, fidgeting with my necklace and sipping the wine. It burns my throat in a way I welcome. "She needed my fear, and what is fear, but the belief that something is dangerous? I stopped fighting. I didn't run. I suppose, I stopped believing she could harm me, and so, she could not. I don't know if she died, or if she simply disappeared. But she left the bow behind."

He glances at the artifact hungrily. "So this is the fabled Twilight Bow. The weapon that will pierce the darkness. Can you feel it humming? It yearns to be used."

Sure, I guess. I mean, it does exude a sort of power. "We'll use it soon enough on the rider. But first, we need to find the Shadow Mantle. Any ideas of where it may be?"

He turns his head to the side, staring into the calm water of the pool. "There is one place. The tomb of my uncle, Lord Levi, Prince of Envy. He ruled this castle before me. He believed vampires should be the only race to govern Inferna, and for his beliefs, he died in the Midnight War. It was before my time, of course, but I have learned many stories of the man. There is one I think most important."

He continues talking, but I need to keep my hands busy, so I cut off a piece of my rugged cloak and tie it around Theo, making a pouch. I place the little wolf cub within, petting his head. "There... now Theo doesn't have to carry you in his mouth all the time."

My little manticore purrs in acknowledgment.

Duke likes his new pouch, as evidenced by a wagging tail and contented pup settling in for a rest.

"This tale is known by only a few," continues Elias, looking my way. One of his eyes appears to ripple in the light, like a pool of sapphire water. "But it was told to me by my father. You see, most see Levi as a solitary figure, but he did not seek to be so. For millennium, he sought to produce a natural heir. A baby born of his blood. With many women he tried, but every attempt ended in a stillbirth. In Inferna, such things are an ill omen for royalty, said to bring famine and death upon the land, and so Levi kept his wives and their dead children a secret from his people. Thousands of corpses he burned. Thousands of babes that never lived.

"One wonders if at some point it was his duty to stop. If it at some point he became responsible for the deaths." Elias tilts his head to the side. "They say, if you listen closely in these parts, you can still hear a baby crying on the wind."

I try to listen, but I hear only our breaths. I wrap my arms around myself, shivering. "So, nice ghost story and all, but what's your point?"

"My point, First Hunter, is thus: If the dead could speak, they would tell you of their pain. And of the rotten place this world has become."

The wolf pup falls out of his pouch and runs up to Elias, sniffing at his hand. Then he jumps back to my side, whining and shivering.

I look upon the man with the tattoos. The man with piercing blue eyes.

"You're not Elias," I spit, grabbing the Twilight Bow and jumping to my feet.

He freezes. And then his lips curl up in a dark smile. "Took you long enough, First Hunter."

ARIAS

*T*he creature stands before me. A perfect replica of Elias. Even now that I know it's an illusion, I cannot make out the signs. "How is this possible?" I whisper. "How can your spell seem so real?"

He tilts his head, cracking his neck. "There is much you do not understand, First Hunter. But I can show you." He holds out his hand.

Without thinking, I draw the bow, and even though I have no arrows, a light appears in my palm. A gleaming arrow. I aim it at the imposter's heart. "You're the one who framed Elias for the massacre."

He chuckles. "It did make him easier prey. When he went on the run. Away from all those he loved. I almost caught him then. That is, until you showed up."

"Where is he?" I hiss. Theo growls behind me, turning to full size, his silver tail whipping through the air.

"He is where I want him," says the imposter, pacing around the pool of water. "Soon, he will be dead. And the Unseen Lord will return."

"Take me to him," I yell, pulling the bow tighter. "Take me to Elias. Or I swear, I will kill you where you stand."

He chuckles darkly, and wisps of white drift around his body, covering him in armor. It twists around his body like a second skin. It covers his head like a true face. When he speaks again, his voice is both low and a whisper. "You may try, First Hunter," says the White Rider. "You may try."

I fire at him.

He draws a sword where there was none a moment before. A blade of moonlight. And cuts through the arrow.

I fire again and again, projectiles of light appearing from thin air each time I need one, but he rends them all in half, and they dissipate into harmless smoke.

"We both possess a piece of the Shadow's Bain," he says, spinning his sword. "One will not overcome the other."

His words build a rage inside me. A madness waiting to break.

I fire again.

He blocks once more. "Very well," he growls. "If you seek battle, then I shall oblige." He leaps forward, closing the distance between us.

I fire again, but he spins away from my attack, lunging forward with his sword. He will tear into me. The same way he did Callie.

He strikes.

And Theo dashes in front of me, taking the blow into his own shoulder. He roars with a pain that shatters my heart, collapsing into the pool, his blood mixing with the water.

"No!" I roar. And something snaps inside.

The darkness the witch showed me. The monster within.

I charge forward through the air, my feet not even touching the ground as I accelerate, shadows gathering in my wake, and slam into the rider like a spear, ramming us both across the room and through a window. We explode into the light, struggling in the sky as we fall toward a lake. I grip his arms in my hands, and try as he might, he cannot escape my grasp. We are about to fall into the water, but then the pool freezes below us, and we crash into ice instead, finally tearing apart.

"Where did you take Elias!" I roar, and my voice is not my own. It is a thing both primal and raw. Full of darkness and pain.

"I sensed the moment you dispatched the nightmare," he says as we circle each other. Two predators on the prowl. "I took him while you recovered on your knees, still grasping at the illusion. So easy it was, to finally capture my prey."

I toss the Twilight Bow over my shoulder and draw my dagger. It extends with steel black as night, growing into a sword. "You will find it's not easy at all, rider."

I close the distance between us, striking faster than I ever have before. He blocks my attacks, and for a moment, we are a perfect pair, dancing on the pond, the ice freezing below our steps. The light begins to flicker. As if the sun itself is going out. The world becomes torn in two. Half-shadow. Half-light. We leap between the two sides, exchanging identical blows, swapping places back and forth. He cuts my arm lightly. I slice his leg.

"You fight for the wrong side, First Hunter," he growls. "The council will never accept you. Your uncle, if he ever learns what you are, will fear you. And Elias... the Elias you seek so hard to save. If he knew your true nature, he would detest you. Perhaps he does so already."

"But let me guess, you'll accept me for who I am?" I ask, kicking his knee.

He stumbles back. "I understand what it is to be unwanted. To be the monster everyone fears."

"Unlike you, I don't kill children."

He pauses, frowning. "Children? Ah, you speak of the song. First comes the frost. Second the flame. Third are the voice of those he has slain." He chuckles. "You actually think I'm the creature from legend? The rider on the steed of snow? Truly, do you still not recognize who I am?"

I strike quickly three times, but my blows are slower than before. "You almost made me believe the lie, but that's all it is, isn't it? A ruse? A part you play?"

He nods. "Well done, hunter. Well done. I do pretend to be the rider. For it is so much easier to have your way when people fear your very name. But tell me. How long does one need to pretend, before they finally become the thing itself?"

The more we fight, the more our moves become sluggish, but we remain tied. I punch him in the gut. He head-slams me in the nose. Doesn't break it though. At least, I don't think.

The flickering shadow fades, while the sun remains in full force. My hands turn sweaty around my sword. My chest grows heavy. It's not long before I'm faltering.

The rider stumbles as well, driving his sword into the ice and leaning on the hilt. "This is futile," he says, his deep breaths ragged.

I swing at him with a tired hand. "Give me back Elias, and we can stop fighting."

He blocks clumsily. "That, I cannot do."

"Why?" I spit. "So an eternal darkness can fall upon the land? So vampires may rule all the worlds?"

He sighs, falling to his knees. "Too long has my kind been treated like beasts. Too long have they been starved like animals."

"So, you're a vampire?"

He chuckles, but there's no humor to his voice. "You disappoint me, hunter. I thought you would have figured out the truth by now."

I draw the Twilight Bow and fire an arrow at his helmet. "Care to show me?"

Even tired, he manages to deflect the projectile. "Perhaps. Maybe then you will understand." He clutches the armor at his neck, undoing a clasp. "Many years ago, the High King and Queen made a mistake. They tried to hide their secret. But they failed." He grips his helmet and pulls it away.

I...

I don't understand.

His face.

It must be an illusion.

He looks like Elias once more.

But...

How can his magic be so powerful?

Unless...

Unless it's not magic at all.

Unless this is his true face.

And then I understand.

"You're his twin," I whisper.

The rider drops his helmet. His face shimmers, and one eye turns green. His hair turns light. A scar forms across his nose. "Now you understand," he says, and his voice sounds almost exactly like that of Elias. "I need but bits of illusion to look like my brother."

My legs buckle beneath me. "No... this can't be... I would have heard of another prince."

He bows his head. "When the Queen became pregnant a second time, she gave birth to not one child as expected. But two. Both boys. One healthy and strong. The other malformed and crippled. The weak child did not make it through the night. In Inferna, such births are an ill omen to the people, and so, after advice from their council, the king and queen decided to keep the second birth a secret. Only their closest friends learned of the babe. The father, Fenris Vane, wanted to burn the child, as is the vampire custom. But the mother, Arianna, wanted a burial, as was the way of both Fae and humans, her ancestors. In the end, they dug a small grave under a tree and lay the babe in the earth. And then they left him to rot."

The rider scowls. "But the babe was not dead. Not truly. He awoke in the night and crawled out from the earth. He fed on the worms in the dirt and made his way to the river for water. There he found a woman, or rather, she found him, and she took the child as her own. She brought him home to her husband, and together they named him Arias, after the stars."

He stands, looming over me. "For years, I knew nothing of my birthright. But as I aged, people began to notice similarities between me and the young prince. And then, someone came to kill me in the night. I fought them off, but not before they killed my father. At least, the man I called my father. I stabbed the assassin in the heart with his own blade, and I knew then my very existence was a curse. So I left home. And I wandered. Until I finally discovered my purpose." He points the blade at my throat. "I will burn the old Inferna away. And in its place, a new kingdom will rise. One where the mistakes of the past are not repeated over and over again. One where my people, vampires like my father and mother, will finally have peace."

I try to stand, but my feet buckle below my weight. My hands turn numb. "I will stop you," I say, my voice barely a whisper.

"Don't you see, First Hunter?" he asks, sitting in front of me, his different colored eyes meeting mine. "I won this fight before it even began."

I try to raise my sword, but my hand falls limply at my side.

And then I remember.

The wine.

He drugged me.

But…

"You drank as well."

He grins. "I developed an immunity to such things long ago, girl."

I try to reach into my cloak for an antidote, but my arms are too weak.

The rider brushes my cheek gently with his hand, and his face seems so innocent. So comforting. So much like the prince I know. "Sleep now, Iris. For when you awaken, everything will be made clear."

My eyes begin to close—

Something grabs me from behind. Yanks me back.

I fall into a pair of arms, looking up at a face covered in shadow.

"You will not have her, Arias," says the newcomer.

And then we are in the air, flying into the clouds, the rider disappearing below.

DREAD PRINCESS

J wake with a raging headache. Like seriously, is renewal back up yet? Because I need to cut this head off and get a new one. Let's see... nope. Still need to wait about a quarter of a day. Wait a second, how did I die again?

My memory is fuzzy. Like... Callie kept me up all night partying fuzzy. But this doesn't look like home. Strange.

I sit up in a bed of soft linens and take in my surroundings. A humble cabin. Nice. Windows letting in daylight: check. Cozy fireplace: check. Creepy boiling pot: check. Mysterious bottled herbs on shelf: check. Totally not suspicious cloaked figure sitting in corner: check. Okay. Okay. If movies taught me anything, I'm either, One: waking up after a wild one-night stand, probably married to the handsome stranger over there, or Two: I've been kidnapped and am about to be tortured and possibly eaten. Again. Either way, I'd rather not stick around to find out, so time to get up and—

"Be careful," yells the stranger. A woman, I realize.

Her warning comes too late.

I tumble out of the bed, collapsing face first into the hardwood floor. Ouch.

"The drug still hasn't worn off," says the mysterious lady, rushing to my side and helping me back into bed. Her hands are soft like a baby's butt. Her voice reminds me of hot chocolate. Can it be?

She pulls off her hood, smiling at me, and her silver hair—half braided, half wild—falls past her shoulders, framing her ashen face. Red flames flicker in her emerald eyes.

"Aya?" I whisper, my voice weak, my lips cracked and bleeding.

The princess, AKA Elias's sister, nods. She grabs a handful of herbs off her shelf (at least, I'm assuming it's her shelf) and crushes the leaves with a mortar and pestle, depositing the mixture into a pot of liquid steaming on the fire. With a wooden ladle, she fills a clay cup with the concoction, then offers the potion to me. "Drink this. It will help with the headache."

I eye her suspiciously, slowly taking the beverage in my weary hands. I can't remember last night or this morning, but I sure remember the princess. "Last time we met, you betrayed me."

She rolls her green eyes. "I was playing a part. Why else would I save you from the rider?"

The rider!

Memories come storming back.

"The rider has Elias," I say hurriedly, setting the cup down on a side table. "I need to save him. They're brothers and—"

"I know," Aya whispers somberly. "I know about Arias."

"But..." I can barely think right now. My brain is on fire and over-loading with information.

The princess sighs, walking back to the table and mixing a new batch of herbs. "I was around for their birth. I saw the dead babe. I saw the burial." She slams down the pestle hard. "Like everyone else, I was sworn to silence. I was but a little girl, and yet I had to keep the death of my baby brother a secret."

Blah, blah, blah. "Tragic story and all, but you missed the part where I have to go." I point at the door and try to stand and— Oh, right. I can't. "New plan. You save Elias."

"I can't—"

"You saved me, didn't you?" Though... how? I remember flying, but vampires can't fly, unless...

I whistle.

And kitten Theo bursts through the door, leaping into my arms and purring. Duke follows next, jumping onto the bed and curling up next to my legs. He's bigger than I remember, up to my knees in height now.

Aya smiles with unbridled affection. "They've been guarding the door all day."

I scratch them both behind the ears and notice the bandage on Theo's shoulder. "You treated him?"

Aya nods. "Of course. I'd be screwed if it wasn't for him." She tosses the new herbs into the pot, fills up a cup, and sips on the drink herself. "I arrived just before you passed out. I was ready to fight Arias, but he began conjuring an army of frost. I was about to be overwhelmed when a manticore swooped down from the castle, carrying, of all things, a wolf pup in a pouch, and swept us into the air."

"Good boy, Theo," I say, petting him under the chin. I turn back to Aya. "How did you find me?"

Aya leans back in her chair, crossing her legs on the table. "After you 'escaped' my ship, I kept hunting you as per the council's orders. Unbeknownst to them, I always stayed two steps behind. Far enough to keep my crew from intervening again, close enough to help in a real emergency. My vessel, the Dread Shark, was on the lake near Crimson Castle when you and the rider fell from the fortress and onto the water. You were far away, of course. I had to use a spyglass to see the details, but when I realized you were in trouble, I grabbed a boat and made my way to you, leaving my scheming crew behind."

Her story sounds legit, but it doesn't mean she's not working for the council. (I mean, she's a member, after all.) She could have other plans in store for me. But Theo seems to trust her, enough to be calm around her anyway. And Duke jumps in her lap and starts licking her cheek. He seems to like her instantly, the same way he liked Elias. And he didn't like Arias. So that's something.

I glance at the cup on my side table. It could be some kind of sleep potion, but then again, if that were the case, why let me wake at all? Maybe I'm being a fool, or maybe my head just hurts way too much and I need relief, but I take the potion and drink. Not a sign of complete trust, but a step in that direction.

Aya glances at me, sipping her own drink, and for a moment, we share an understanding. We'll do anything to save Elias.

I look around for my gear. My dagger lies on the table. The Twilight Bow lies on the mantelpiece. The rider didn't get it. Good.

Aya follows my gaze to the legendary artifact. "To be honest, I wasn't sure you would find the bow. Elias always believed in the Shadow's Bane, but I thought it more myth than reality. Seems you proved me wrong."

She stands, adjusting the silver clasp on her black cloak, and walks over to the mantelpiece, hovering her hands over the silver bow. It hums under her fingertips. It sparkles in her eyes. "Any idea where one can find the Shadow Mantle?" she asks curiously.

I shake my head. "No. Besides, I doubt we have time to go looking."

"I suppose you're right." She pulls away from the Twilight Bow, and for a moment, it seems hard for her to leave it behind, but leave it she does, sitting back down in her chair. She opens her mouth, as if to say something, but then her lips close, and she hums a melancholy tune instead.

"Where are we anyway?" I ask.

"A safe house of mine. In the Outlands. In the middle of nowhere, really. We should be hidden from Thalius and his followers here."

So basically, she doesn't want to disclose our exact location. Whatever. Theo could bring me back if needed.

"Listen," I say, clasping my hands together. "The rider is going to use Elias's blood to free the First Vampire. The deal is—"

"I'm familiar with the legend," she says quickly. "Have been for some time. But... why Elias's blood? They're twins. Why does Arias need someone else at all?"

"No clue. Maybe he needs something more than just a bit of blood. Maybe he needs..." I clench my jaw. "A life."

Aya grips the side of her chair, her nails tearing into the wood. "I see... but if he already had Elias, why try to take you as well? Why not just leave?"

I shrug. "Could be he just wanted to make sure I won't stop him." It's a lie. Because I suspect he had more sinister reasons. Reasons I don't quite yet understand.

I take a deep breath, focusing on what I do know. "If the First Vampire is freed, an Eternal Night will fall upon Earth. We're talking Armageddon level shit here."

She grabs the rapier hanging on her hip. "Then we have no time to waste. Any idea where they went?"

"I…"

Shit.

"Silence," I whisper. "You back yet?"

I never truly left.

"Right so—

"Are you talking to yourself?" asks Aya, examining my head. "Quick. How many fingers am I holding up?"

"Three. And no, I'm talking to a demon inside my mind. Duh. Now, hush."

I use my quiet voice again. "So, creepy demon. Any idea where the White Rider took Elias?"

To unlock the Unseen Lord, says Silence. *Yet he has not done so yet. I am not sure why…*

"Right. But like, *where* did he take him?"

This even I am not privy to. But you must find him. Find him before it's too late.

So that's useless. "Where were you before, anyway? Could have warned me about the rider masquerading as Elias."

I was indisposed.

"Why?"

Why is not important. Only Elias is important.

Fine. Sure. I turn my attention back to the princess, raising my voice to normal levels. "Well, I know we can find them at a giant tree. I'm talking a massive piece of shrubbery. Like a Mother Tree, if you've ever seen one, except this one looks dead and rotting. Sound familiar?"

The princess shakes her head. "There's only one tree I care about in Inferna. The place we buried Arias. But it's not the thing you describe. After all, aren't Mother Trees a myth?"

"They're no myth," I say seriously. "I've seen one. Sly says there's only one per world. He says…"

I pull out my leather notebook, AKA what my cellphone transformed into, and flip through the pages, eventually landing on sketches of a grand tree, with roots spanning an entire world. I drew these myself, by the way, in case you were wondering. Oh, except that image. That really cool water painting used to be a photo in my phone. Anyway, point is…

"Sly says all Mother Trees are connected. Mirrors of each other. Bridges between worlds."

I show the princess my journal, and she studies the sketches skeptically. "So you're saying, if we find one Mother Tree, we may find another?"

"Yeah. Kind of."

She sighs wearily. "I'm not sure…"

"But I am." I grit my teeth and force myself to stand. My legs wobble, but they don't collapse. "I'm going after Elias. You can come or stay behind."

She lowers her head. "You care for him, don't you?" she asks, twirling a silver ring on her finger.

"I…" My throat tightens. "I still need to bring him in. He still needs to face an honest trial."

For some reason, she chuckles at my response. "Right. Sure you do." Then she jumps to her feet. "So, where's this Mother Tree you saw?"

"We need to get to my house," I say. "Are there any mirrors nearby? Or—"

Aya pulls out a pocket watch and flips it open, revealing a small looking glass within.

I frown. "But I thought mirrors in Inferna were rare and heavily guarded."

She shrugs. "This mirror is rare and I'm guarding it. What can I say? There are perks to being a princess." She smiles mischievously.

All right, one problem solved. Now for the second. "You can only travel somewhere you've been, right? So take me as close to the Valley of Silence as you can—"

"I've visited your house. Back when it was abandoned. I..." Her words trail off, leaving things unsaid. "How about we stop talking and get out of here."

Right. Let me just completely ignore that mysterious aside. She's lucky Elias is in danger right now or else... wait, I guess she's not so lucky, huh?

I stride (more like stumble) over to the fireplace and throw the Twilight Bow over my shoulder. I retrieve my dagger from the table. Theo and Duke curl around my legs, making physical contact, and I grab Aya's hand in my own.

"Ready?" she asks.

I nod. "When we save your brother and the world, I expect a promotion."

"Clear your name first, then we'll see."

I look up innocently. "You know, if you die on this mission, it will be a complete accident. And in no way related to me trying to take your seat on the council."

She laughs.

And we flash into the mirror.

MOTHER TREE

*W*e appear in, of all places, my bathroom, right next to the mirror. The space is decked out, of course, with marble walls and a top of the line Jacuzzi tub. But it's not exactly spacious, squishing Aya and I together. "After you," I say, clearing my throat and gesturing to the door. She nods and walks out, Duke and Theo following at her heel. I go next, kind of excited to be back home after all the crazy started. Let's see—

Are you freaking kidding me?

The place is totaled.

A complete mess.

Someone went through all my stuff. Even cut my precious red couch open. Probably Thalius and his goons. I just hope they didn't find my secret.

I rush to one of my handmade tapestries, depicting a battle between High Queen Arianna and Oren, an ancient Fire Druid. There's a cool story there, but right now, the important part is what's behind the tapestry.

Carefully, I untie the fabric from the ceiling, speaking as I work. "Did you know your brother was the rider?" I ask.

"No," says the princess. "I knew he lived. I discovered the fact many years ago. But I only figured out he was the rider when I saw the two of you fighting on the lake."

Okay but… "If you knew the truth, why keep Arias secret?"

"It was not up to me. Not truly." Her eyes drop. "I spoke to him once. Many years ago. I asked him to take his rightful place as Prince of Hell, but even then, he was lost to vengeance. He swore to destroy the High King and Queen. And with everything going on in my kingdom, I fear he may have succeeded."

"You mean…"

"I mean the Queen and King may not be lost. I mean they may be dead at the hands of my brother. At the hands of the rider." Her fingers tighten around the hilt of her rapier. "I worry we are too late to save even Elias."

"I don't think so," I say gently.

"How can you be sure?" she snaps.

Because when Elias fed off my blood, he changed. And though his vampirism returned when I died, I feel a part of me still runs through his veins. The rider is waiting. Waiting for my effects to wear off entirely, before he sacrifices the Prince of Darkness to the Unseen Lord. Why else has the Eternal Night not begun?

I wish I could say these things to Aya, but then I would have to explain my blood, my heritage, and that I can't do. Not to her. There isn't enough trust there yet. So instead I say, "Elias is no easy target. Believe me, I would know. Only took me twenty-two times to finally catch him. And even then, he managed to slip away."

She nods, a hint of a smile returning to her lips.

"When we find the rider," I continue, "and we will find him, we still need a way to defeat him."

"Think the both of us can't handle him?" she asks.

I gesture down at my fickle legs, though they are doing much better. "I'm not exactly in top fighting shape here. Probably won't be for another day. And you're good but, no offense, not as good as me."

She chuckles. "Is that so?"

"I've studied every keeper on the council. Looked through the reports. Your days as a hunter were impressive, no doubt, but I still hold the record for most successful hunts. After you apply the appropriate algorithms, taking into account monster levels and mission time, of course."

"Of course," says Aya, rolling her eyes. "So, what's our plan then, oh mighty record holder?"

I shrug. "Don't have one. Not yet anyway. But I'm sure I'll think of something."

The tapestry falls to the ground, revealing a brick wall.

Aya frowns. "So, what are you doing again?"

"Patience, princess. Patience." I run my hand against the stone, trying to remember the right spot, ah, here it is. I press down on the brick, and the wall swings inwards, revealing a secret passage.

The princess raises an eyebrow. "I didn't find that when I was last here."

"Took me years to find it myself. But it's been here the entire time." I pause, briefly glancing out the window. My three llamas, Wit, Smarts, and Brains, graze under the moonlight peacefully. Thank goodness they're okay. Someone from the Black Lotus must have kept an eye on them for me.

"Don't worry," says Aya, nudging my shoulder. "I made sure they were provided for."

"Wait? You?"

She grins. "Your llamas are innocent, are they not?"

"Well, yeah. Though I do suspect Wit steals food from Brains sometimes."

She chuckles.

Make haste, yells Silence. *Your time runs short.*

"Yeah. Limping along as fast I can here." I shake my head, walking through the secret passage and into a stone tunnel.

Aya looks at me oddly as she follows. "When you said you were talking to a demon in your head, you weren't joking, were you?"

"Nope." I show her the mark on my wrist. "I touched something weird and boom. Telepathic link with a demon."

"And you trust this thing?"

"Nope."

She nods once, sharply. "Good. My mother made a deal with a demon. An unbreakable blood oath. It took her through hell. Literally. For a while, I suppose you could say things ended well, but look at the situation now. She's gone. And the realms are in chaos. Raiders burning villages. Warlords conquering castles. I fear it will get worse before long."

"Unless the High Queen returns," I add. I do hope she's alive. I mean, she's like my hero. My role model. Like, real model, not weird teen crush Thalius role model. She's who I want to be when I grow up. Yes, I'm already grown up, but you know what I mean. Arianna Spero, the Midnight Star, brought peace between Fae and vampires after millenniums of war. She slayed a dark King. She was pretty young too, so we have that in common. They wrote a biography about her, you know. Vampire Girl. You should check it out, little bird, unless of course you already have.

So, where was I? Oh right.

We're here.

The passage expands into a massive cavern, the inside of a hollow mountain.

And at its center stands a white tree with crimson leaves.

Its branches reach high into the sky, lit by beams of moonlight falling through cracks in the stone. Its roots sprawl across the entire chamber, like lines of fabric woven together in intricate patterns. Glowing mushrooms grow on the bark, and fireflies swirl through the air. There is little sunlight here, and even less water, and yet the Mother Tree stands strong, swaying in a breeze that isn't there. If you close your eyes, and listen to its movements, you can almost hear it speak.

"So they *are* real," whispers Aya.

I nod. "I found this one a few years after moving into the valley. I brought Sly here later, though I got the sense he had already been here before."

The princess steps forward, placing her hand on the tree. "So how do we travel from here?"

I shrug. "No clue. Though..." I look at the massive statues that surround the chamber: nine people, all of different shapes and sizes and races. Each of them blindfolded. I don't know their meaning or their purpose. However... "There was a door," I say, walking up to the statue near the entrance. "A door near the Dead Tree that the rider used. If the same door were to be in this chamber, I reckon it would be about here. Right where this statue is."

Aya rubs her chin. "So is it an illusion? A puzzle? A—"

I whistle and Theo grows to full size, tackling the statue, shattering it apart, revealing an open gateway in the rumble.

"Or maybe we just do that," says the princess, nodding along.

"Question is," I say, examining the runes, "How do we activate it?"

Aya walks up to my side. "I don't recognize these markings, but they remind me of the Waystones in Inferna. Those passages need blood to function."

"Care to volunteer some?" I ask. "After all, you do have the special royal Midnight Star blood, right? Which reminds me, why isn't Arias after you?"

She tightens the clasp around her cloak. "Perhaps he thinks I'd be harder to catch. He would not be wrong."

I suppose that makes a certain kind of sense.

I draw my dagger, offering it to her. She rolls her eyes and bites into her wrist instead, then smears her blood on the runes. Oh look, one's starting to glow. And another. The gateway begins to hum, the center glowing blue. Wow. This is actually working—

The light fizzles.

The sound fades.

Guess I spoke too soon. "Maybe it just needs more blood," I say.

Aya shrugs. "Then add yours."

Might as well. I prick my finger with my dagger and—

"Seriously?" asks Aya. "That's it?"

"Hey. Not all of us have super healing." Until I can use renewal again for a new body, that is. It should be up in a few minutes.

I press my bloodied finger against a rune, standing next to Aya. Each of us fuels one side of the gateway, and the markings begin to glow once more. The humming returns. The blue light starts to glow again.

"Step away from the portal!" yells a familiar voice. A voice I most hate.

Thalius.

He stands at the entrance to the chamber, twelve watchers and hunters at his back. His white fur cloak hangs from his shoulders, and he wears the Mittens of Justice. Oh sorry. The Ravagers. They're called the Ravagers.

"What a fool you were to return home, girl," he hisses. "Did you not think I'd have someone watching the house? I knew the moment you stepped inside."

"Yeah, actually I did think that," I say casually. "But then I thought, it's only Thalius."

He growls, raising his claws.

Aya pulls a blue vial from her cloak and tosses it to me. "Take this. It'll return your strength. Fix your legs."

"And you waited till now to give this to me?" I ask, downing the liquid.

"It will only last a short while." She pulls away. "Once the portal is working, use it to find the rider. Use it to save my brother."

"And you?"

She grins. "I'll be fine." And then she turns toward Thalius, drawing her rapier. "You may not believe I'm as good as you, Iris, but I'm better than this ass."

"What is this, Aya?" he hisses, his silver-blue hair shining in the moonlight. "You're helping the girl?"

She makes a shocked face. "Aiding and abetting a known criminal? Never. I'm just conducting my daily training session. Right here in this chamber. I'd be careful about getting too close. Sometimes, it's as if my sword has a mind of its own."

Thalius scoffs. "Take the both of them into custody, watchers."

No one moves.

"Watchers?" he asks, glancing backwards. "Hunters? Do as I say, or I will banish you from the Order."

Still, no one moves.

"I'm sorry keeper," says a small Fae woman. "But both you and Aya are on the council. We can't fight her just because you say so. Code: 123 specifically states, the council must rule to demote a keeper, before action can be taken against them."

Thalius growls, turning back to Aya. "As I recall," he says. "The code doesn't apply to other council members."

The princess smiles, twirling her sword. "And as I recall, last we sparred you ended up crying at my feet."

Some of the hunters giggle.

And an unbridled rage overcomes Thalius. He raises his claws and charges.

The gateway opens.

And I jump through.

As much as I would like to see this fight, the White Rider awaits.

I fall into a world of snow and darkness. A world of cold and death. I whistle for Theo, but he does not come. The gateway is closed. The light gone. It seems our blood was enough only for one passenger.

Very well.

Aya's potion has kicked in, fueling my muscles with strength, and I stay low, creeping toward the Dead Tree, searching for my opponent and Elias. I find the White Rider near the top of a hill, standing in his pale armor, his face uncovered, his light hair drifting in the furious wind. Everyone has a final challenge. And he's mine.

FULL NAME: Arias Vane Spero

Classification: Half Vampire / Half Fae

Title: The White Rider

Physical Description: six feet tall, light hair, pure muscle, scar across the face, one eye blue, one eye green (heterochromia)

Level: 1000 (seriously he is too strong)

Possibly poisoned my uncle.

Definitely kidnapped Elias.

Wanted for being one evil son of a bitch.

BASTARD BETTER BE READY. Because I'm coming for him.

UNSEEN LORD

*T*o be honest...
     I'm afraid.
Of losing to the rider.
Of never clearing my name.
Of never saving Sly.
And you, little bird.

I'm scared you won't believe my story. I'm scared you'll read these words and think them a lie, an elaborate ploy to make me seem the hero. I'm worried you'll call me a thief, a fake, a failure.

But I am none of these things.

I am strong.

I am clever.

I am me.

Iris the First Hunter.

And the tale that follows is as true as can be.

* * *

ELIAS IS TRAPPED in a cage of ice, as if he were hit by a wave and the water froze with him in it. Only his head is free. Perhaps so he could breathe. Or maybe so he could talk. His eyes are closed, the lashes frozen over, and he doesn't seem to notice me.

The rider walks up to him and takes a long sniff. "Finally," he says, his voice rumbling. "Your blood has returned to what it once was. It is time." He waves his hand, and the ice prison melts, dropping Elias face first to the ground.

And then I see his back.

The deep cuts there.

The rider tortured him.

The Prince of Darkness makes no attempt to stand. His eyes open sluggishly.

And meet mine.

I wink.

The smallest hint of a smile appears on his face, and he looks to the rider. "You know, I'm still not sure we're twins. I mean, I'm just so much more handsome than you. And you lack my charm entirely—"

"Silence!" yells the rider, slapping his brother across the face.

Elias chuckles, spitting blood on the snow. "See? My point exactly. No class."

He's distracting him. Giving me a chance to strike.

Well, here it goes. I close my eyes and take a deep breath, focusing my mind. I draw the Twilight Bow and take aim, my hands steady. This is my one chance. My one advantage over him. I can't miss. I must pierce his armor. I must end him in a single shot. I count to three.

One…

I target his heart.

Two…

I hold my breath.

Three…

I fire.

The rider spins at the last moment, and my arrow takes him in the shoulder instead. He roars, clutching at his wound, his eyes finding me. "Hunter!"

"Sorry not sorry," I yell, firing again.

He draws the Moonlight Sword, cutting my arrows of light apart. "You're a fool to face me again."

A blizzard begins to storm around us. Soldiers of frost crystallize before me, protecting the rider. I fire at the creatures, shattering them with my arrows. But for each I destroy, two more appear in their place.

The rider chuckles, grabbing Elias by the collar and dragging him through the snow. Dragging him toward the Dead Tree.

I fire at Arias, hoping to slow him down.

But one of his soldiers leaps in the way, absorbing the blow and shattering into a thousand pieces. Crap. I need a new plan. Maybe—

A sword of ice slashes toward my arm.

I dodge, drawing my dagger, and cutting down my attacker. Two more soldiers strike at my sides. I leap backwards, and they smash into each other, exploding into shards of ice.

Think, Iris. Think. I'm running out of time.

The rider pulls Elias to the base of the tree. He smashes his hand onto the imprint.

The Prince of Darkness yells, his blood seeping into the ashen bark, covering it with patterns of crimson.

Arias looks down at his brother's pained face, and for a moment, I see him pause. "It will be over soon," he says somberly. "Then you can finally rest."

Lightning flashes in the sky.

Thunder booms in the distance.

The Dead Tree pulses, beating like a heart. The roots begin to weave and slither. They pull back from the center of the tree, opening, and within, I see a red light.

"And so his reign begins," says the rider. "The First Vampire. The Unseen Lord. Has returned."

The opening grows, the tree cracking, splintering apart.

Elias faints. He is dying. Almost completely devoid of blood.

I need to stop this. I need to break free.

But the soldiers are too many. They come upon me in the dozens, clouding my vision, pushing my reflexes to the limit. One cuts me in the leg. The other in the arm. I snarl, my dagger extending into a blade dark as night, slashing through three creatures at once. Ten more charge at me. I tear past them. Twenty more. I crush them. Thirty more. I shatter them all. And yet they don't stop. They keep coming. They won't kill me. But they'll keep me at bay. Long enough for Elias to die. Long enough for the Unseen Lord to break free.

And that, I realize, is the problem.

"Hey rider!" I yell, my sword becoming a dagger once more. "Guess what?"

"What?" he groans, turning away from his precious tree.

"You can't win!"

"Really?" He chuckles. "Why?"

"Because…"

I raise my dagger.

And stab myself in the heart.

"Because I'm the First Hunter, bitch!" I yell from the sky, my new body plunging straight down toward the White Rider.

Before he can even look up, I drive my dagger into his neck, collapsing on top of him. He lets go of Elias, and the prince's hand falls free from the tree, feeding it with blood no longer. The creatures of ice shatter, and no more rise in their place.

I grab the Moonlight Sword from the rider, pointing it at his throat.

"No," mutters Arias, his voice barely a rasp. He pulls the dagger from his neck, staining the snow beneath crimson. He tries to reach for his brother once more.

I step on his fingers.

They crack.

The White Rider screams.

And for the first time, I see fear in his eyes.

"Please," he whispers. "Please. I must finish the ritual."

I sheath the Moonlight Sword in my belt and pull the Twilight Bow from my back, taking aim at the center of the tree. I count to three.

One…

I target the heart.

Two...

I hold my breath.

Three...

I fire.

And the arrow of light pierces the tree, setting the bark on aflame, an unnatural scream echoing through the night.

"No," hisses the rider, crawling forward. He places his own hand on the rune, letting his own blood flow into the roots.

I rush to pull him away, but the fire lashes downwards, setting his hand ablaze. It spreads up his arm, consuming his body.

I wrap my hands in my cloak, reaching for him, but something snaps up above, and a flaming branch falls toward us. I jump backwards, grabbing Elias and rolling out of the way, as the log crashes down between us and the rider. The blaze turns into an inferno, and embers fill the sky. I can barely see Arias past the flames. But I can hear his screams.

Elias stirs in my arms. "It's too late for him," he whispers. "It's too late... for my brother."

He stills, his body limp. I look down at the handsome prince and startle at his deathly pallor as I realize it's almost too late for him as well. The thought quickens my heart, and there's no hesitation as I slice open my arm and hold it over his mouth. He doesn't fight me this time. He's too far gone.

In fact, he doesn't move at all.

"Damn you, bastard. Drink. Don't die on me now."

The seconds tick by.

The tree continues to burn.

My blood flows over his lips, down his chin, dripping into his mouth, but still he lays lifeless.

Tears burn my eyes as I will him to drink. To feed. To live.

After what feels like an eternity, something flickers on his face. His teeth elongate and sink into my flesh. Hands reach for me, holding my arm against his mouth.

He drinks.

He feeds.

He lives.

I pull away before he can drain too much of me. He is still weak. Still close to the edge. But he will live.

I lift him into my arms and turn away from the burning tree, carrying Elias down the hill.

I grasp the iron key around my neck. And as I open the gateway back home, the sun begins to rise.

TRIAL

*D*isclaimer: The rider and I may or may not have actually had that badass exchange right before I stabbed him in the neck. I mean, I was fighting like a hundred ice creatures. I didn't have time to chat. But I said those things in my mind. So that counts, right?

So what next?

Do I turn in the Prince of Darkness?

Do I set him free?

Well, if you've read the public records of my trial, you're already privy to the important parts.

I returned the Moonlight Sword to the Council of Hunters and turned myself over to the authorities.

I was charged with theft, assault (of Thalius, specifically) and escaping the Black Lotus dungeon. (Which had never happened before, so there was some confusion over what the punishment should be.)

Aya, the Dread Princess, testified on my behalf. She said she witnessed the White Rider wielding the Moonlight Sword and fighting the First Hunter (that's me) with her own eyes. Thalius called her a liar, of course, and told his own version of events. In his story, I poisoned my own uncle, released a paralyzing airborne toxin within the Black Lotus, and at some point lost to him in an epic duel only to escape somehow. Since he had zero evidence or witnesses (excluding himself), his accusations were quickly dismissed. Not to mention, Sly himself testified I wasn't the poisoner. Nor was it Elias, my so-called accomplice. So who was it?

Well, the council pinned the blame on the White Rider. But, personally, I suspect Thalius. He hates me and Sly. Has aspirations beyond his station. Plus, he just looks guilty, you know? I want to vomit every time I see his face. Do I have any proof? Not yet. But I will someday.

In the end, all but Thalius voted in my favor, and the council declared me innocent of all charges. Yay!

Sly was released as well and restored to his rightful place as Emperor of the Black Lotus (a title he totally made up, but when you're as old and as powerful as him you get to do shit like that). I asked him more about my heritage, but he adamantly stuck to his original story.

I'd like to say our justice system is awesome, but if I hadn't retrieved the sword, I'm pretty sure I'd be in a cell right now. There's still corruption to weed out. Council members to replace. Changes to make. Mysteries to unravel regarding Lix Tetrax and the Unfettered. But many of these problems will have to wait until I make keeper, and that's still a long way off.

After the trial, Aya returned to Inferna, determined to find her parents and restore order to her realm. She offered to take me with her, but I'm better suited to hunting criminals than deciphering politics. Still, sometimes I hear a rumor about the High King and Queen, and I always send the tip her way.

Sadly...

Callie never returned. Sly worries the White Rider got to her, but she's too clever for that. Personally, I like to imagine she's on a beach somewhere, drinking thousand-dollar champagne while a dozen men and women cater to her every whim. I'll find her one day, I suspect, but only when she wants to be found.

From Silence, I never heard another word. Probably because we won.

And as for Elias…

Well, you already know what I told the council. "I tried to arrest him, but I was too injured after my fight with the rider, and he was too fast, and he got away for the twenty-third time. I totally swear he did."

But as for what really happened.

That's just between you and me, little bird.

2 MONTHS LATER

This isn't what it looks like. I swear. You see, though I may be playing a highly illegal game of dice and bones, and yes, though I may be losing an unfathomable sum of money, I am in complete control. Utter domination. You get the picture. All children and sensitive souls may read on.

But wait, Iris, you may be saying. What about those three old crones, Iris?

How kind of you to be concerned.

But those beautiful witches shuffling the cards and tossing the dice are no problem. There's Al'Kallach, the Kind. Ma'Ga'Ta, the True. And Jane... the um, well there's actually a ton to say about Jane, to be honest. But perhaps the most important is she finally forgave her mother.

They call themselves the Three Sisters, because while they were performing community service and going through rehab, the trademark finally went through. Now I know what you're thinking. Iris, where did you learn all this? You don't hang with that kind of crowd, but you're wrong. I do. Because Elias was right. There is beauty in all things. Even semi-reformed criminals. And we've been chatting for the past three hours.

"Sorry again about the whole cooking you and eating you thing, Iris," says Al'Kallach, dealing the cards. "We were going through a hard patch, but that's no excuse. What we did was diabolical."

"Absolutely horrible," adds Ma'Ga'Ta.

"And delicious, I mean terrible," finishes Jane.

I nod sagely, staring them each in the eyes one by one over my hand of cards. "I forgive you. But you know... if you really wish to make it up to me, you could start losing a round or two."

They exchange glances. "Nah," they say in unison, starting the round with a roll.

"So ladies," I say, leaning forward. "I'm looking for this bloke, recently back in the game, if you catch my meaning."

Jane turns away, blushing. "I haven't seen any bloke."

"Now, Jane," I say softly. "Remember your motto."

The crones turn to each other and recite in unison. "Justice before crime. Good before evil. Three Sisters forever."

"Maybe we should start a superhero team," muses Al'Kallach.

"Or a band," suggests Ma'Ga'Ta.

"All good ideas," I say, "But about this fellow. He's on the list, ladies. You just don't want that kind of drama in your life, am I right?"

"Here, here," says Al'Kallach, and we all clank our champagne glasses together.

"So Jane?" I ask. "What's it going to be?"

She smiles sheepishly. "Oh, alright. He's upstairs." She adds smugly. "In my new room. Fifth door on the left."

Bingo.

I toss my cards down on the table. Four skulls and a rose.

The crones can't believe it. "How?" they mutter.

"All about patience, ladies," I say, pulling the pot of chips toward me. "Come to mama."

The Three Sisters are still scratching their heads when I leave them at the table and head upstairs through the cavern. So walking... walking... ah, I reach the redecorated corridor. A picture of Buffy next to a painting of Dracula? Nice. Anyway, I'm alone here. Not even

Theo accompanied me on this particular mission. The door's right in front of me.

I just have to reach out and turn the handle. But my hands are sweaty. My heart is beating fast.

Then—

"We meet again, hunter!" roars Imenath from behind me. Silver armor clads his entire body. Horns sprout from his helmet.

"Hey buddy," I say, turning around and drawing my trusty daggers. "Ready to continue the epic battle? The never-ending conflict?"

He sighs, lowering his giant mace. "Imenath tired. Imenath know you seek another."

"Actually…" I say, stepping forward. "I'm here for you, buddy."

His eyes light up. "You mean?"

I reach into my cloak and pull out my shiny new badge. "By my authority as First Watcher, you are under arrest."

That's right, little bird. You heard right.

Your girl, Iris, got a promotion. Aya pulled some strings after the whole saving her brother thing, and with my top-notch record, the council finally had no choice. Of course, I started off as watcher one thousand fifty-seven or something, but after a few missions, taking into account my prior successes, and applying the proper algorithms, I quickly shot up to number one.

"You've been busy these last few months, stealing all that chocolate," I say, putting the badge away. "Number two on the list, by the way."

He beams, his eyes tearing up. "Number two? You mean…"

"It's a new record, buddy. Congratulations."

He nods, wiping his tears and raising his mace. "Then… Imenath the Terrible, number two on the most wanted list, will destroy puny watcher."

He swings his giant mace with all his might at my head. To some, like Imenath himself, perhaps this would be a fierce and swift blow. But to me, well, it moves at a moderate pace. What can I say?

I'm the First Watcher, bitch.

I punch him in the face, and he flies through the air, crashing through a window down the hall, falling, his voice echoing on the wind. "I will return…"

I should probably follow him. Take him into custody and all that…

But I do have an unfinished matter.

I didn't lie to Imenath. I'm here for him.

But I'm also here for someone else.

I take a deep breath and open the door.

And there he stands.

Elias Vane Spero, High Prince of Hell.

Dressed in a black vest with silver buttons and leather pants that hug his assets just so. Not that I notice such things. Of course not, little bird.

His eyes meet mine.

And he smiles.

"I worried you wouldn't be here," I say softly.

He chuckles. "And miss our first date? Never." He raises the glowing match in his hand, and finishes lighting an assortment of scented candles around the room. With the mood set, he gestures to a table set for two, complete with a wide array of cheeses and meats and desserts. "I hope you like crone cooking," he says, sitting down across from me.

I look at the man before me. At the kindness of his face. The play-fulness in his eyes. To be so close to him again is to feel alive in a way I cannot describe. To feel like nothing else matters but this moment. "Elias, I—"

"Let me stop you there," he says, holding up his hand. "Before you say what I know you're about to say, know this: Coming here wasn't a mistake. Letting me go two months ago wasn't a mistake. What we have between us, whatever this may turn out to be, is no mistake. But…" He holds out his wrists. "If you've changed your mind, if you wish me arrested, then I will come with you without a fight. And that too, will be no mistake. Because I trust you, Iris. I know you will do what is right. Better than I ever could."

His words make my heart flutter. But… "Actually, I was just going to ask you to pass the salt."

He blinks. "Oh, in that case. Here you go. But I meant what I said, Iris. I trust you completely. I don't expect you do the same with me. In fact, that'd be foolish. But I hope one day, you may be able to."

"I hope so too," I say, smiling as I take a bite of cheese. I notice the bed of furs next to the fireplace. "A little presumptuous for a first date, isn't it?" I ask.

He shrugs. "I like to be prepared." With a wink, he grabs a champagne bottle out from a bucket. "Care for a drink?"

"Actually," I say, pushing back from the table. "If you don't mind, I'd like to hop in the shower for a sec. The journey here left me a little dusty."

"I don't mind at all, love," he says casually, popping the bottle open with ease.

"Pour me one while you wait," I say while sauntering away. Well, I try to saunter. Never quite got the technique down.

I find the bathroom and pull off my leather gear and lay down my weapons. (Including the Twilight Bow, which I totally kept in secret.) A red dress falls out of my cloak. The one I snuck in for later. I hang it on a hook and step into the shower, reveling in the warmth of the water as it runs down my body. Despite myself, I can't help but think back to the last night Elias and I saw each other.

I carried him through the gateway, taking him to my old room at the Black Lotus. Not the safest place for us at the time. But hey, I only had two options. The Valley of Silence, where I'd just seen Thalius, or the hotel, where I knew all the secret passages. So the Lotus it was.

I lay Elias down on my red couch, propped his head up with a pillow and wiped the excess blood from his mouth. He was so weak, barely conscious, despite having just fed off me, but he was alive. I remember sitting down by his side, holding his hand, just enjoying his company as the minutes ticked by.

And then they came.

Watchers knocking on the door.

I knew I had to make a choice.

And so I grabbed a mirror from my dresser and placed it in Elias's weak palm. And I leaned down and whispered in his ear. They were words only meant for him. Words I will not repeat, even here. Not yet, anyway.

He looked deep into my eyes, gently caressing my face with his hand. "Iris…" he said softly.

And then I pressed my lips against his.

Tasting him.

Feeling him.

His lips cool. His breath sweet.

For a moment, our bodies melding together. Our passion all consuming. He smelled of pine and earth. He felt like home.

And then it was time…

I pulled away. Elias and I shared a final smile. And he vanished into the mirror.

I opened the door to the watchers, and well… you know how the rest goes.

It wasn't long until the Three Sisters called me up with an apology. Something about seven steps to acceptance. Anyway, they wanted to say sorry in person, and so we met over dinner (which did *not* include human meat this time, I assure you). Which soon turned into a game of dice and bones. Which soon turned into a bit of a weekly occurrence. Though they still apologize every single time. It wasn't until our second meeting, when they slipped me the note.

Meet me here in two weeks' time—E

I struggled over the decision for days, but in the end, I simply thought: What would Callie do?

And so I'm here. Talking a shower and about to slip into one sexy red dress. On a date with a criminal. Who would have thought? I still didn't bring heels though. I mean, it's not like I'm a completely different person. I—

The shower runs cold.

Wow. They really need a better water heater. Like—

A chill creeps over my skin.
Frost gathers on my hair.
No. It can't be.

> *He'll come in the night*
> *In armor of white*
> *Riding a steed of snow*

I jump out of the shower, grabbing my bow.

> *Three signs there are*
> *That mean he's not far*
> *Silver army in tow*

I rush naked back to the living room. Back to where I left Elias.

> *First comes the frost*
> *Second the flame*
> *Third are the voices*
> *of those he has slain*

I leap into the cavern, nocking an arrow of light. But I'm too late.

The candles flicker silver. The White Rider stands over the table, holding a silver sword to Elias's throat.

My throat catches. "How? I saw you die."

Arias chuckles deeply, gazing into me with his emerald and sapphire eyes. White armor clads his body. But his face he keeps visible. "You are not the only one who can escape death, hunter," he says, pressing his blade into his brother's skin until he draws blood. "It took me months to recover. But recover I did."

"Stop!" I yell.

"Don't worry about me, love," says Elias. "Shoot the bloody bastard. By the way, this isn't how I imagined seeing you naked for the first time, but you look marvelous. Definitely worth the wait—"

"Shoot and he dies," growls the rider. "Unlike us, he will not come back."

I hesitate.

And that's all the rider needs.

He throws the prince at me.

I barely lower my bow in time, the arrow almost piercing Elias' chest, and we crash to the floor together. Before I can get back up, the rider grabs my arms. Steel wraps around my wrist. Trimantium shackles engraved with runes. The same ones Sly wore in the dungeons.

"Kill yourself this time," hisses Arias. "And your magic won't save you."

"Let her go," yells Elias, jumping to his feet. He rushes for me, but a wave of water rushes up behind him, trapping him in a prison of ice. The water from my shower, I realize. Somehow the rider can control it.

"Why are you doing this?" I ask. "The Unseen Lord is dead. Your mission is over."

He flips me around so we're face to face once more. "When you left me to burn by the great tree, I saw deep within the roots. I saw the truth. And now, I know what I must do."

"You want revenge on me?" I snap. "Fine. Take me. But leave Elias. You don't need his blood anymore."

"No," says the rider, looking at his brother. "I suppose I don't." Then he raises his silver sword.

And cuts open the prince's neck.

I scream.

Something hits me on the head.

And I fall into darkness.

SILENCE

*W*ake up.
       Wake up.

Wake up.

I WAKE IN THE NIGHT, staring at a trail of snow. My lips are cold and broken. My throat is parched and aching. My limbs are sore, dangling in the air, and I realize I'm on the back of a horse, tossed over the saddle like a sack of meat.

I try to examine my surroundings, but my neck is stiff and my body tied down. I can make out a forest, though. Grey trees as far as the eye can see. And snow everywhere.

My clothes are...

Well, I'm wearing clothes, for one. Not my own. But black furs and a dark cloak.

Someone dressed me.

And that someone must be the rider.

He sits beside me on the white steed, his armor glimmering in the moonlight.

I should have known he would return, says Silence. *I should have warned you.*

"You're back," I whisper, hopefully so quiet the rider won't here. "Where were you?"

I thought our battle was almost over. I was wrong. The rider can't be slain by normal means. But you will defeat him. We will find a way. We will—

"He killed Elias," I snap, my voice cold.

Yes, says Silence. And for once, the deep voice sounds sad. *He did. But he will do far worse if you don't stop him. If you don't fight.*

I don't want to fight. I just want to rest. And sleep. And—

Wake up.

My eyes open.

Your body is shutting down in the cold. You must tell the rider.

"Why would he care?" I mumble.

He needs you alive. I will explain later. Once we are face to face.

"Face to face?"

Yes. You are close to me now. We shall meet soon.

"And then?"

Then... then I will explain everything.

I clench my jaw, straining uselessly against my shackles. If I die with these on, I die for real. No renewal. A part of me welcomes the end. To fall from the horse at such an angle as to snap my neck. To finally rest. To see Elias again, if such things are possible. But another part... the louder part... howls for vengeance. There will be time to mourn what almost was. First, Elias's killer must pay.

"Hey rider," I whisper. "Rider!"

He looks over his shoulder, staring at me with his green and blue eyes, his light hair drifting in the wind. "What do you want, hunter?"

"Too cold," I say, so numb I'm not even shaking. "Too cold..."

"You will be warm soon enough," he grunts. But I see a hesitation in his eyes. He raises his hand, whispering words of the ancient Fae, and warmth spreads through my veins.

"Did you..." I start, my voice louder than before, "Did you warm my blood?"

He grunts, saying nothing.

I move my fingers, clenching and unclenching my fists. "I will kill you, you know."

"You already did once," he spits.

Then the moonlight fades, and I realize we're entering a cave. We ride deep below the earth, until torches of silver flame begin appearing on the walls. Finally, we stop, and the White Rider dismounts. He unties the ropes that bind me to his steed and drags me off the horse.

When I fall into the dirt—my body about as useful as a limp dishrag—he yanks me up by my shackles and pulls me over to a wall, wrapping chains around my manacles, securing me in place.

"If you try to run, there will be pain," he says plainly, and then he leaves, disappearing into the shadows with his steed. The light dims with their departure, and I realize he must have the Twilight Bow in his saddlebags. Why wouldn't he?

The spell he cast continues to work, warming me from within as my eyes adjust to the darkness. I'm in a cave, that much is clear. The ceiling is quite high, so high I can't make it out in the shadows. I'm chained to a wall of rock. Not much different from the Black Lotus dungeons, to be honest. More spacious actually. So how do I escape?

"Any ideas, Silence?" I ask.

"Yes," comes a voice.

But it's not in my mind.

It's right in front of me.

Something rattles in the dark, and a figure crawls forward in the dirt, chains falling from their shackled hands. Their limbs are thin and withered. Their skin is plagued with sores. A dress that was once white but is now dirty gray covers their small body. And a mop of wild black hair hides their face.

"Silence?" I ask, frowning.

"Yes," she whispers, her voice soft and delicate, so unlike the one I heard in my mind. "I am Silence. But you may also know me by another name."

She raises her shoulders, pushing back her raven hair, looking at me with emerald eyes.

That face...

I've seen it before. In my books. In my studies with Sly.

She looks around my age, and yet I know she is not.

"You're..." My throat catches. "You're Arianna Spero. The High Queen. The Midnight Star."

Her lips curl into a smile. "A pleasure to finally meet you in person, Iris."

"You've been here all this time," I say, realization dawning on me.

She nods. "When I learned my son had lived, I sought him out. I did not know he had already become the rider. I did not know that when I found him he would take me prisoner. I did not know he sought to awaken the First Vampire." She pauses. "But I did what I could to stop him. I sent my mark to help you. To guide you. I wish I could have told you more, but as I said, our link was not secure. I had to keep certain truths hidden from you. Certain truths I, myself, have only begun to understand."

I crawl forward, as far as I can anyway, to sit across from her. "But why me?"

"You are one of the few who can stop my son," says the Queen. "Maybe the only one. I suspected your importance from the beginning, but you are far more powerful than even I imagined. Even Arias did not fully understand what you are. Not at first."

"What do you mean?" I ask, my chest pounding. "What am I?"

She lowers her head, her green eyes filling with tears. "I am so sorry, Iris. I am so sorry for what is to come."

"Tell me everything," I snap. "Tell me why the rider wants me alive."

"Don't you understand? You're the one he's been searching for."

"What?" My blood runs cold. My hands tremble. "What do you mean—"

"The tale? The legend? It was wrong." Her voice is soft, as if speaking to a frightened child. "It wasn't their father the two brothers cursed, but another. For their father had a third child. A daughter. And to her he promised all he owned."

No...

"The brothers, fearing to lose all they sought to inherit, cursed their baby sister, locked her away forever. Until someone found her. Someone freed her."

No...

"They left her at the Black Lotus."

No...

"Now you understand, hunter... You are the First Vampire. You are the Unseen Lord."

EPILOGUE

Written by Elias Vane Spero

So, I'm alive. That's the good news. My sister, Aya, found me before it was too late and fed me her blood. She's been keeping an eye on me, apparently. How sweet.

Now the bad news.

"Iris is the Unseen Lord," says Aya, as we sit in the captain's cabin of her ship, the Dread Shark, drinking goblets filled with blood. Duke naps by my legs. He is already taller than my knees.

"That makes no sense," I reply. "She's been in the Earth Sun. She doesn't drink blood."

"Don't you remember the legend?" she snaps. "Burn her they did. Starve her they did. And yet she would not die." My sister stands, pacing back and forth. "Don't you see? The first curse went terribly wrong. It didn't create a vampire like us. It didn't weaken her in any way. It just made her stronger."

She smacks her hand down on the table. "If she were to feed on blood, she would be more powerful than you can possibly imagine."

This can't be…

And yet.

When I fed on her blood, I knew she was different.

I knew she was special.

"She took away my curse," I whisper, clutching my fist. "When I fed on her."

Aya nods. "Yes and no. I suspect she cannot remove the curse. Not entirely. But she can make us more like her. She can dull our craving for blood, remove our weakness to the sun. At the expense of our strength, that is. At least for a while."

I look into her eyes. "How do you know all of this? How can you possibly know?"

She sighs, sitting back down and taking my hands in her own. "Because I learned the legend long ago, dear brother, and Lix Tetrax came for me as they did for you. For years, I worked to keep the Unseen Lord locked away, rising through the ranks of the Order, but then someone freed her. They left her at the Black Lotus as a babe, but she began to age naturally. I didn't realize what the girl was at first. But as the years went on, I began to suspect. It wasn't until I saw her duel Arias on the lake, the sun flickering in and out, that I realized what she truly was."

I push her hands away, standing up. "I am part of the Order, same as you," I say. "The Unseen Lord was trapped in the Dead Tree. I saw him burn."

"Did you? Or did you imagine you did?" she asks quietly.

"I… I'm not sure. I…" I thought I felt a presence, but perhaps that was only the tree.

"Iris *is* the Forgotten One, the First Vampire, the Unseen Lord," says Aya. "And now the White Rider will use her to bring upon an Eternal Night. He will use her to cover the nine worlds in darkness and give vampires rule over all other races."

I turn away from her with a scowl. "You knew this, and yet you told me nothing."

She sighs. "You weren't exactly around, dear brother. Long ago, I accepted we walked different paths, and I sought to give you the freedom to travel yours."

"But you tell me now," I say, letting the venom drip from my voice. "What changed, great princess?"

She flinches, her face suddenly sad. "You began to care for her. I had to tell you."

I shake my head. "We need to find Iris," I growl. "We need to save her."

Duke senses my mood and stands, baring his teeth, ready to fight at my command.

"Don't you understand?" asks Aya softly. "She is the Unseen Lord. And once the rider unlocks her powers, she will become our enemy. Not only our enemy, but the greatest enemy the worlds have ever known."

"Maybe yours. And maybe the worlds'. But never mine." I stride towards the window overlooking the expanse of water to our west, the sun setting over the waves. And I think about Iris, about what she would do. "Dum Spiro Spero," I whisper. "While I breathe, I hope."

Iris needs me, and I will find her.

A knock on the door.

"Expecting someone?" I ask.

Aya nods, avoiding my eyes. "There is another matter we must discuss." She raises her voice. "Come in. We're ready."

The door opens.

And then *he* enters the room.

A man with hair dark as night and eyes like the moon and sea. A man with skin pale as my own. He wears a perfectly tailored suit and his nails are expertly manicured. His smile is as smooth as the devil's.

"Uncle Asher?" I ask, my curiosity piqued.

The Prince of Pride steps forward, a leather journal under his arm. "I'm afraid there has been a complication," he says, adjusting his collar. "Your parents have been missing for so long, absent from their duties, that a part of their will has come into effect. A contract sealed in blood. A contract that must be fulfilled."

"Our parents live," I say, walking up to him.

He sighs somberly, looking between me and my sister. "Be that as it may, it's time we honored their wishes. It's time we picked the new ruler of Inferna."

TO BE CONTINUED

Little bird, you're still here! Well, done. This is Iris, btw, in case you were confused, for a little behind the scenes chat. You didn't think you'd be rid of me that easily, did you?

Here's the deal. I was about to get my happily-ever-after-roll-in-the-hay-with-a-sexy-prince-of-hell blablabla when shit hit the fan and now here we are. You must be DYING to know what happens next. I know I am. So head over to ReadKK.com and sign up for the newsletter there. I've been told by the magical powers that be this will notify you as soon as the next chapter of my story is ready. If you're on Earth, look for an email. If you're anywhere else, look for a messenger pigeon or some shit. It takes time to be this witty, so be patient, if you can manage.

And while you wait, you may remember I mentioned the biography of the great Queen Arianna Spero, Midnight Star, aka Elias's mother. Totally worth a read. Go there now and check it out, cuz you're def gonna want to be caught up on her story as this little saga continues. Just search Vampire Girl by Karpov Kinrade. There are four books, so don't be lazy.

If you've already blown through your history lessons, then get ready to ride dragons in Of Dreams and Dragons. This is an epic saga that takes place on one of the nine worlds, so you're not going to want to miss it. You know the deal. Search the title by Karpov Kinrade and you should be good.

And don't worry, little bird, I'll be back soon. Nothing keeps Iris, First Watcher, down for long.

Peace out.

ABOUT THE AUTHOR

Karpov Kinrade is the pen name for the husband and wife writing duo of USA TODAY bestselling, award-winning authors Lux Karpov-Kinrade and Dmytry Karpov-Kinrade.

Together, they write fantasy and science fiction novels and screen-plays, make music and direct movies.

Look for more from Karpov Kinrade in *Vampire Girl*, *Of Dreams and Dragons*, *The Nightfall Chronicles* and *The Forbidden Trilogy*. If you're looking for their suspense and romance titles, you'll now find those under Alex Lux.

They live with their three mostly teens who share a genius for all things creative, and six cats who think they rule the world (spoiler, they do.)

Find them online at KarpovKinrade.com

Or on social media @KarpovKinrade

* * *

If you enjoyed this book, consider supporting the author by leaving a review wherever you purchased this book. Thank you.